AIR ALERT

RESCUING
THE EARTH'S
ATMOSPHERE

W9-CNA-836

BOOKS BY CHRISTINA G. MILLER
AND LOUISE A. BERRY

COASTAL RESCUE:
Preserving Our Seashores

JUNGLE RESCUE:
Saving the New World Tropical Rain Forests

ACID RAIN:
A Sourcebook for Young People

AIR ALERT

RESCUING THE EARTH'S ATMOSPHERE

CHRISTINA G. MILLER AND LOUISE A. BERRY

ILLUSTRATED WITH PHOTOGRAPHS AND DIAGRAMS

ATHENEUM BOOKS FOR YOUNG READERS

Atheneum Books for Young Readers
An imprint of Simon & Schuster Children's Publishing Division
1230 Avenue of the Americas
New York, New York 10020

Book design by Virginia Pope
The text of this book was set in Berling.

Printed in the United States of America
First Edition
10 9 8 7 6 5 4 3 2 1

Library of Congress Cataloging-in-Publication Data
Air alert: rescuing the earth's atmosphere / by Christina G. Miller and
Louise A. Berry.
p. cm.
Includes bibliographical references and index.
Summary: Describes the earth's atmosphere; discusses air pollution, the greenhouse
effect, and the theory of global warming; and presents a vision of an energy future.
ISBN 0-689-31792-1
1. Air quality management—Juvenile literature. 2. Air—Pollution—Juvenile litera-
ture. [1. Air—Pollution. 2. Pollution.] I. Berry, Louise A. II. Title.
TD883.13.M55 1996
363.73'92—dc20
95-21295
CIP
AC

Note to the reader: All temperatures cited in the book are in Fahrenheit.

Dedicated to the survival of the polar bear
(*Thalarctos maritimus*)

ACKNOWLEDGMENTS

We would like to thank the following people for being valuable resources to us as we researched material for this book:

Dr. Chung S. Liu, D. Env.
Director, Applied Science and Technology
South Coast Air Quality Management District, California

Massachusetts Audubon Society
Dr. Elizabeth Colburn, Aquatic Ecologist
Hatheway Environmental Resource Library
Ms. Margaret S. Mariner, Librarian

Dr. John S. Perry, Director
Board on Global Change
National Research Council

Dr. Susan Solomon, Senior Scientist
National Oceanic and Atmospheric Administration

CONTENTS

Clouds are part of the beauty of Earth's atmosphere. CREDIT: SCOTT N. MILLER

CHAPTER ONE

THE ATMOSPHERE—EARTH'S FRAGILE ENVELOPE OF AIR

Earth's **atmosphere** is made up of a special combination of **gases**, particles, and tiny water droplets. This mixture makes our planet the only one in our solar system, and perhaps in the entire **universe**, where life exists. We are dependent on this invisible atmosphere for every breath we take. We cannot live without its air for more than a minute or two. Without our atmosphere, we would have no beautiful blue skies, fluffy white clouds, or colorful sunsets. No matter where we live on Earth, we are touched by the atmosphere. A seventeenth-century Italian inventor, Evangelista Torricelli, stated that we live submerged at the bottom of an ocean of air.

In the twentieth century, exploration of outer space has taught us much about the Earth and its atmosphere and the atmospheres of other planets in our solar system. We know that there are four layers of atmosphere that surround the Earth: the troposphere, stratosphere, mesosphere, and thermosphere. The layers are of various thicknesses and are pulled by gravity toward the Earth's iron core.

The troposphere is the thinnest of the layers. It is closest to the surface of the Earth and contains 80 percent of the atmospheric gases. It is where all Earth's weather occurs. The troposphere ends 6 to 10 miles above the Earth depending on how far you are from the equator. As you go higher in the troposphere the temperature drops. Near the top it may be 100 degrees below zero or colder!

The next layer of the atmosphere is the generally cloudless stratosphere. It extends from the troposphere to 30 miles above the Earth's surface. Long-distance jet airliners usually fly in the stratosphere so that they can avoid thunderstorms and snow, which are found in the troposphere. The upper region of the stratosphere is about 28 degrees and looks violet-black. It is warmer than the atmosphere above and below it because it contains the ozone layer that absorbs much, but not all, of the sun's **ultraviolet radiation**. Ultraviolet radiation, among other things, gives us tans or sunburns.

Above the stratosphere is the mesosphere, which extends from 30 to 50 miles above the Earth. The mesosphere boasts the lowest temperature in the Earth's atmosphere, 135 degrees below zero. In sharp contrast, above this layer is the thermosphere, which begins about 50 miles from Earth and continues far into space. The thermosphere is completely exposed to the sun's radiation, and temperatures in the upper part of this layer can reach 2,700 degrees. The exosphere is the outermost part of the thermosphere. It is very thin and contains so little air that it is almost like a **vacuum**, a space in which most of the air has been removed. The exosphere extends about 300 miles above Earth and gradually fades into interplanetary space.

It was in the seventeenth century that the first accurate understanding of the atmosphere was gained. Scientists then built the first crude instruments to measure temperature,

Layers of the atmosphere as seen from space. CREDIT: NASA

humidity (moisture content of air), and air pressure.

In 1644, Evangelista Torricelli invented the **barometer**, an instrument that measures **atmospheric pressure**, or the weight of the air. Air has weight and is pulled to the Earth by gravity, the same force that pulls a ball to the ground when you drop it. At sea level, a cubic foot of air weighs a little more than an ounce, or about the same as five quarters. If you were to explore the atmosphere, you would find that air pressure decreases as you go up, and there would be less air weighing on you. Also, there is less oxygen as you go higher.

Because all animals, including humans, need oxygen to breathe, you would be gasping for breath and feeling dizzy 2.5 miles above sea level. At 8 miles, there is even less air, and there would not be enough oxygen to survive. To maintain near-normal atmospheric conditions inside the cabin of a jet plane, it is pressurized to Earth's surface air pressure before

AIR ALERT

Because air temperature decreases at higher altitudes, some mountains have snow on them even during the summer. CREDIT: LOUISE A. BERRY

take-off. Flight attendants instruct passengers on how to use oxygen masks in case pressure drops during the flight.

As you travel away from Earth the temperature of the air decreases just as the air pressure does. The heat from the sun in absorbed by the Earth and transferred to the surrounding air. As the heated air rises, it expands because of the lower pressure. This expansion cools the air, just as the air escaping from an automobile tire feels cool. This explains why some mountain peaks have snow on them even during the summer.

Earth's atmosphere, its animals, plants, oceans, and fresh water are all part of a balanced system that is powered by the sun. The sun provides energy for green plants, trees, and crops to grow. In a food-making process called **photosynthesis**, plants remove carbon dioxide (CO_2) from the air and give off oxygen (O_2). Animals, including human beings, are dependent on oxygen for life. They breathe in oxygen and breathe out carbon dioxide. These two opposite forces help maintain the delicate balance of gases in our atmosphere.

You may be surprised to learn that the oxygen we breathe makes up only about 21 percent of Earth's atmosphere. Seventy-eight percent of the air that surrounds our planet is nitrogen (N). Carbon dioxide makes up only .04 percent of the atmosphere. It is one of the "trace" gases, meaning gases that are found in very small quantities.

About three and a half billion years ago Earth's atmosphere was very different from that which surrounds our planet today. Then it contained large amounts of carbon dioxide. The earliest forms of life on Earth were **bacteria**, simple one-celled organisms that can be seen only through a microscope. More than one billion years ago simple plants that lived in the sea grew and multiplied. Then an important

Plants remove carbon dioxide from the air and give off oxygen in the process of photosynthesis. CREDIT: LOUISE A. BERRY

change occurred. The oxygen the plants gave off as a result of photosynthesis built up and started to form part of the air we breathe today. As millions of years passed, plants began to grow on land and fish-like creatures began to grow in the seas. The atmosphere changed to one of less carbon dioxide and more oxygen, and different forms of life evolved on Earth.

Geologists, scientists who study rocks and minerals, know that the Earth is almost five billion years old. They call the period of the existence of the known universe "geologic time." This time is divided into periods of from 50,000 to one billion years. Dinosaurs lived in the Triassic Period of geologic time. They roamed the Earth for nearly 200 million years from 225 million years ago to the end of the Cretaceous Period, sixty-five million years ago. By comparison, human beings have inhabited the Earth for the very briefest of time, about 300,000 years.

The way geologists learn about plants and animals that lived long ago is by studying **fossils**. These are the remains of dead plants and animals. Fossils are preserved in rock formations. As dinosaurs and other prehistoric animals and plants died, their remains were covered by the sea and layers of sand and mud. Over millions of years these earthen layers turned into sandstone and limestone. Their weight squeezed the moisture from the prehistoric plants and animals and they became coal and oil. This is why coal, oil, and natural gas are called **fossil fuels**.

Fossils also give clues about Earth's ancient **climate**, the average weather conditions over a long period of time. Because at times the climate was warmer than it is at present, plants such as palm trees that now grow only in the South grew all over the land area that was to become the continental United States. What is now New York State had a climate similar to that which exists in Florida today.

While continuing to study the Earth, geologists and

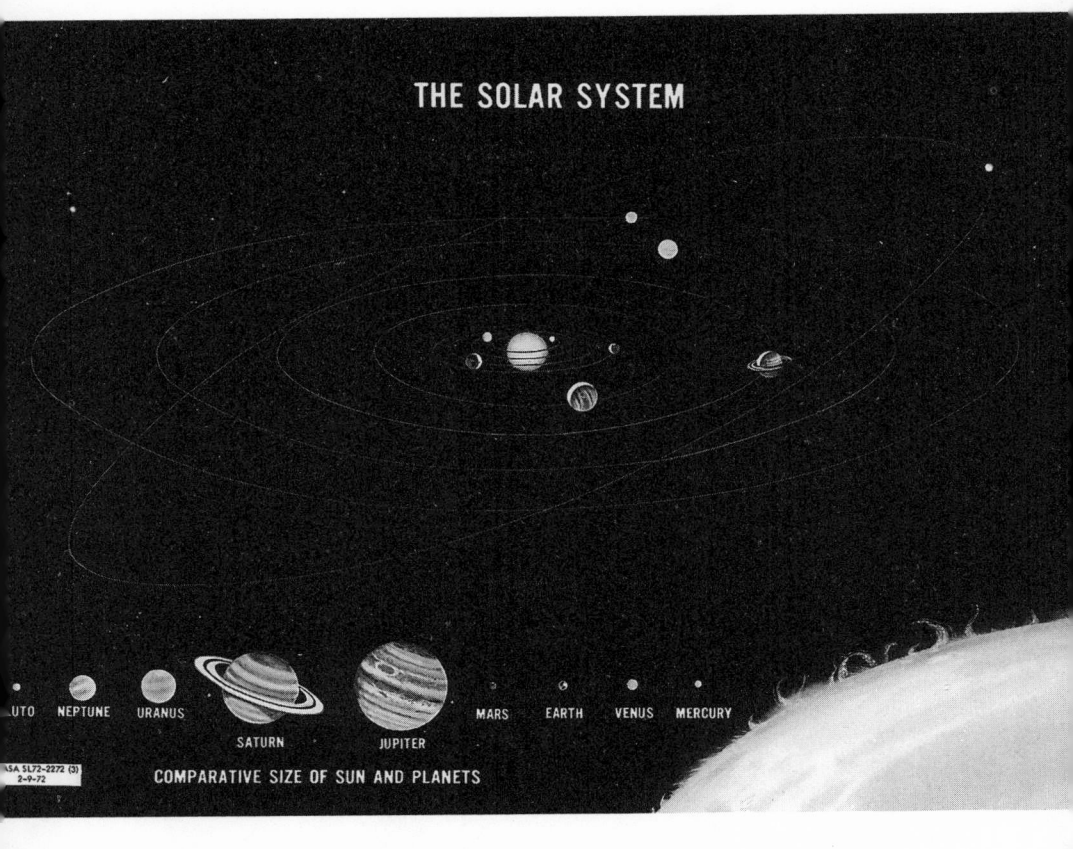

THE SOLAR SYSTEM

PLUTO NEPTUNE URANUS   SATURN   JUPITER   MARS   EARTH   VENUS   MERCURY

NASA SL72-2272 (3)
2-9-72

COMPARATIVE SIZE OF SUN AND PLANETS

The planets orbit around the sun, the center of the solar system. Mercury is closest to the sun, followed by Venus, Earth, Mars, Jupiter, Saturn, Uranus, Neptune, and Pluto. At the bottom of the photograph, the sizes of the planets are shown relative to the size of the sun in the lower right corner. CREDIT: NASA

atmospheric scientists are striving to learn more about the rest of the solar system. Beginning in the early 1960s, the United States and the then Soviet Union sent unmanned probes journeying through space to get close-up views of the planets in our solar system. From these probes we have learned that the atmospheres of the other planets are very different from Earth's. The atmospheres of both Uranus and Neptune contain flammable gases as well as Helium (He), the light gas we

When astronauts landed on the moon, they wore bulky space suits similar to this one worn by an astronaut working outside the Space Shuttle Endeavor.
CREDIT: NASA

sometimes use to fill balloons. Venus's atmosphere is made up of carbon dioxide and wispy yellowish clouds formed from a strong poisonous substance. Mercury has practically no atmosphere and Mars has a thin atmosphere of carbon dioxide that forms **ice caps** of dry ice. Pluto, the most distant planet, has not been approached. Because they have no oxygen, the atmospheres of these planets could not support life as we know it.

American astronauts landed on the moon in six separate voyages between 1969 and 1972. Their footprints remain undisturbed there for the moon has no atmosphere and therefore no wind or rain. While on the moon, the astronauts carried oxygen so they could breathe and wore bulky space suits to protect them from the sun's heat.

Earth's layered atmosphere shields us from the sun's damaging ultraviolet rays, which among other things gives us tans or sunburns. And it is our blanket, helping us to keep warm, at night. It also absorbs water from the oceans, carrying moisture to faraway places, replenishing lakes and rivers.

The atmosphere has maintained itself and life on Earth for millions of years. This fact has given rise to the controversial Gaia **hypothesis**. A hypothesis is something that is not proved but for the sake of argument, or for the purpose of further study, is assumed to be true.

The idea of Gaia, of Earth as a single living organism, dates to ancient times. Gaia comes from the Greek word *Ge*, meaning "Earth." Gaea was the Greek goddess of the Earth. When we speak of "Mother Earth" we are acknowledging our own dependence on the Earth to meet our needs. The concepts of Mother Nature and Gaia are very similar.

But here the scientific hypothesis of Gaia and mythology surrounding Gaea, the goddess, part. The Gaia theory encompasses the idea that the living things in Earth's air and ocean and on its land—form a complex that can be seen as a single system that has the capacity to keep our planet a fit place for life.

The Gaia hypothesis was developed in the 1970s by British scientist Dr. James Lovelock, while working on a National Aeronautics and Space Administration (NASA) project with an American biologist, Dr. Lynn Margulis. He found that Earth's atmosphere is continually replenished by the living things on our planet, and it could not maintain itself without them. From this, Dr. Lovelock put forth the idea that Earth is more than a core of molten rock, plants, animals, oceans, and atmosphere. It is a coherent system of life, like an immense living organism. Its living and nonliving parts work together to slow planetary change, thus helping to maintain the stability of the planet. The Gaia hypothesis implies that changes in climate could be controlled by the living things on Earth, which would be able to modify the atmosphere in order to keep it a fit place for life.

There is considerable scientific debate surrounding the Gaia hypothesis. However, it may help us understand the relationship between Earth's nonliving parts, such as the atmosphere, and the kind of life that exists at a particular time. The way Gaia works is by a slow, gradual **extinction** and replacement of species.

Two hundred years ago people relied on burning wood, muscle power, and the force of moving water and wind to meet their energy needs. Farmers chopped trees and burned wood in fireplaces for heating and cooking. Oxen pulled plows through the fields as farm families followed, planting seeds that would produce their food. They used the force of falling water to turn a shaft that rotated millstones for grinding grain. Windmills converted the energy of wind into mechanical energy that was used to pump water and saw wood. Wind and sun dried clothes after they had been scrubbed by hand in a washtub. There was no electricity; people read by the light of candles or kerosene lamps. People traveled in horse-drawn carriages or in ships propelled by the force of the wind filling their sails.

In the last two hundred years human beings have become an extremely powerful force in shaping the global

environment. The consequences of human activity are just beginning to be understood. Since the Industrial Revolution and the invention of power-driven machinery that burns fossil fuels, factories and gasoline-powered vehicles have spewed millions of tons of **pollutants** into Earth's precious atmosphere. This dirty air is often referred to as ground-level air pollution. In parts of the world where tropical rain forests are being cut down and burned, dense clouds of smoke darken the horizon. Many scientists are now warning that these and other human activities are responsible for recent changes in the atmosphere.

When fossil fuels are burned to produce energy, or tropical rain forests are set afire to clear land, carbon dioxide is released. This is one of a group of transparent trace gases found in the atmosphere that we call "greenhouse gases." This group also includes methane (CH_4) (the same as natural gas), and **water vapor** (water in the form of a clear gas). Greenhouse gases absorb heat. The increase in these gases keeps the surface of our planet and the lower layers of the atmosphere warmer than they would be otherwise.

Our dependence on fossil fuels also causes acid rain. This is the term that is used to describe rain, snow, sleet, and fog that is unnatural because it contains too much of a vinegar-like substance called **acid**. Acid rain occurs because of air pollution in the atmosphere. This impure rainwater affects lakes and forests and all the animals that live in them, as well as drinking water and crops. Even bridges, statues, and buildings are being damaged by acid rain.

Another atmospheric problem concerns the layer of ozone that exists high in the atmosphere. Ozone in the upper atmosphere is like a global sunscreen that blocks some of the sun's ultraviolet rays and protects all plant and animal life on Earth. Scientists believe that human-made chemicals are destroying ozone and reducing the amount of it in the upper atmosphere. Although these chemicals are being replaced with safer ones, they were in widespread use for more than forty years in many common objects, including spray cans, refrigerators, and air conditioners.

Most people would not want to return to the lifestyle of their ancestors. They would miss having such conveniences as cars, computers, compact disc players, refrigerators, and microwave ovens. As people in underdeveloped nations strive for a higher standard of living, the problems of ground-level air pollution, acid rain, the greenhouse effect, and the hole in the protective ozone layer will worsen. People in developed and undeveloped parts of the world must work together, learning from one another, to care for the atmosphere. By reading this book, you are taking a big step in becoming informed about ways to rescue the atmosphere.

CHAPTER TWO

AIR ALERT— SMOG AND ACID RAIN

Earth's atmosphere is both a dump and delivery system for pollutants that cause acid rain, global warming, the hole in the ozone layer, and ground-level air pollution. As smoke from cars, furnaces, factories, and office buildings is discharged into the air and carried by the wind, air pollution becomes a local, regional, national, and international problem.

Throughout time winds have mixed Earth's dirty air with clean air and spread out the impurities. But until the Industrial Revolution most air pollution came from natural sources, such as smoke from forest fires, salt particles in sea spray, and gases from occasional eruptions of **volcanoes**, openings in the surface of the Earth's crust through which melted rocks, gases, and ashes are forced out. Rain and snow washed the pollutants out of the air to the ground and the air remained fairly clean. With the Industrial Revolution air pollution greatly increased, overpowering the atmosphere's ability to purify itself.

We have all ridden in the machine that is the single

Exhaust from the tailpipes of many motor vehicles is a major cause of smog.
CREDIT: SOUTH COAST AIR QUALITY MANAGEMENT DISTRICT

greatest source of air pollution in the United States: the motor vehicle. According to the United States Environmental Protection Agency (EPA), driving a car is the average U.S. citizen's most polluting activity. When the weather is cold, you can see the **exhaust** coming out of the tailpipes of cars, trucks, and buses. The exhaust is the steam or gases that are left over as the vehicle's engine burns gasoline to produce power. When scientists study the contents of exhaust they find a number of pollutants, including carbon dioxide, carbon monoxide (CO), nitrogen oxides (NOx), and hydrocarbons. Carbon dioxide is the most abundant and, as you know, it is the gas that causes much of the greenhouse effect. Carbon monoxide is poisonous when inhaled; carbon dioxide is not.

Nitrogen oxides are a combination of nitrogen and oxygen. None of the 78 percent of our air that is nitrogen is used in a car's engine. When a gasoline engine runs, it uses the oxygen in the air to burn the gasoline. The nitrogen is left over. Heat from the engine causes the nitrogen to combine with some oxygen to form nitrogen oxides.

Hydrocarbons are unburned or partially burned gasoline vapors and are toxic. Some hydrocarbon emissions are known to cause cancer. Hydrocarbons react with nitrogen oxides in the presence of sunlight to form ground-level ozone, a dangerous pollutant. Ozone is not emitted directly from the tailpipe but forms from tailpipe emissions.

Ozone can be either friend or foe to living things, depending where it is found in the atmosphere. In the stratosphere it is friend, protecting us from dangerous ultraviolet radiation emitted from the sun. In the troposphere ozone can be harmful. Surface ozone has always been part of the air we breathe. It is one of the trace gases in our atmosphere. However, before the twentieth century, there was so little of it that it posed no danger to living things. In the past century, global ozone levels in the lower atmosphere have doubled. Perhaps you are wondering why the increased amount of ozone at ground level isn't patching up the hole in the ozone layer in the upper atmosphere. This is because ozone is a very unstable gas, meaning that it combines readily with other materials with which it comes into contact. Therefore, ground-level ozone does not remain intact on a journey from troposphere to stratosphere.

Most ozone produced by vehicles is formed from the pollutants in the exhaust system. However, a vehicle's engine and gas tank are also sources of hydrocarbons that produce ozone. When gasoline is exposed to the air, some of it **evaporates**, meaning it changes from a liquid to a gas. You've probably smelled evaporative emissions at a service station when the gas tank of the car in which you are riding is being refilled. This smell occurs because some of the fumes that are always present in the gas tank escape into the air. For this reason, many states require service stations to have special vapor recovery nozzles on their fuel pumps. These nozzles provide a seal between the fuel pump and the vehicle's gas tank so that fewer hydrocarbons escape during the refueling process. Still, every time a gasoline tank is refilled, whether it be for a lawn mower, power boat, chain saw, or snow blower, hydrocarbons escape into the atmosphere.

Another source of hydrocarbons is a vehicle's engine. The vapors are emitted from the hot engine as it runs and even as the car cools down after it is parked.

Ozone is a severe irritant. It causes burning eyes, choking, and coughing, and reduces lung capacity. Many agricultural crops such as soybeans, cotton, and corn are sensitive to ozone. It stunts growth by reducing the plant's ability to produce food by photosynthesis and makes plants more susceptible to insects and diseases. Of the ground-level air pollutants, ozone is proving the most difficult to control in cities around the world.

Ozone is the major component in **smog**, a word that is made up of the first two letters in smoke and the last two letters in fog. Clean fog is composed of fine particles or droplets of water floating in the atmosphere near the ground. Smog is dirty fog, for the droplets have captured smoke, gases, and particles.

Smog is a sort of "atmospheric soup" of pollutants cooked up by the action of sunlight. This thick, brown haze is made of air polluted by automobile exhaust fumes, smoke, and **aerosols**. Aerosols are particles suspended in a gas. They can enter the atmosphere from smokestacks and tailpipes. They also come from natural sources such as volcanic eruptions and sea spray from breaking waves. The aerosols in smog cause respiratory illnesses in people and animals, are harmful to plants, and reduce **visibility**.

Smog develops when the temperature reaches the mid-eighties and there is little wind. When the weather forecaster talks about "hazy, hot, and humid," conditions are ideal. Because smog formation requires sunlight, the process begins during the morning rush hour. During the day, ozone levels can become ten times higher than normal in some urban areas. They peak in the late afternoon and drop at night. In most urban areas, at least half of the nitrogen oxides and hydrocarbons that cause smog come from cars, buses, and trucks.

Visibility refers to the clearness of the air. If air is very clean and dry, we can see up to 100 miles. Aerosols decrease visibility by reflecting and absorbing light. Unfortunately, the air around many cities is very smoggy. In Denver, a brown cloud of pollutants that sometimes hovers over the city prevents workers on the top floor of tall buildings from seeing things at street level. In downtown Los Angeles, a city on the Southern California coast, visibility is frequently only 16 miles. With clean air it would be possible to see more than 75 miles from city skyscrapers to the beautiful green and brown countryside.

Los Angeles, the second largest city in the United States, is the "air pollution capital of the nation." Air pollutants that spew from the city's eight million cars, thousands of factories and refineries, gasoline-powered lawn mowers, and even lighter fluid used to start backyard barbecue grills, hang in the air for days. This is because Los Angeles is located in a valley called the Los Angeles Basin. This basin is encircled by the San Bernardino Mountains to the east and the San Gabriel Mountains to the north. On the shores of the Pacific Ocean, weak near-shore breezes from the south and southwest hold the city's air over the basin.

Afternoon smog in Los Angeles obscures the view of nearby mountains, which were visible in the clear morning air. CREDIT: SOUTH COAST AIR QUALITY MANAGEMENT DISTRICT

Charcoal lighter fluid often used to ignite charcoal contributes to ground-level air pollution. CREDIT: SOUTH COAST AIR QUALITY MANAGEMENT DISTRICT

19

These geographic features of the Los Angeles Basin create ideal conditions for a "temperature inversion." You know that air temperature drops the higher you go in the troposphere. To "invert" means "to turn upside down." In a temperature inversion the normal situation—with temperatures dropping at higher altitudes—is reversed. Air is cooled as it moves over the Pacific Ocean toward the California coast. In most places this layer of cool air is mixed with and spread out by the warmer air over land. But in Southern California weak winds and the blockade of mountains prevent the vertical mixing of air. Polluting particles and gases produced in the city are trapped by the overlying cap of warm air. The longer a period of stable dry air lasts, the more it prevents pollutants from rising to higher altitudes and mixing with cool, clean air from over the ocean. If the pollutants could rise, they could pass over the mountains, cleansing the Los Angeles air.

While Los Angeles air is gradually improving, "smog alerts"

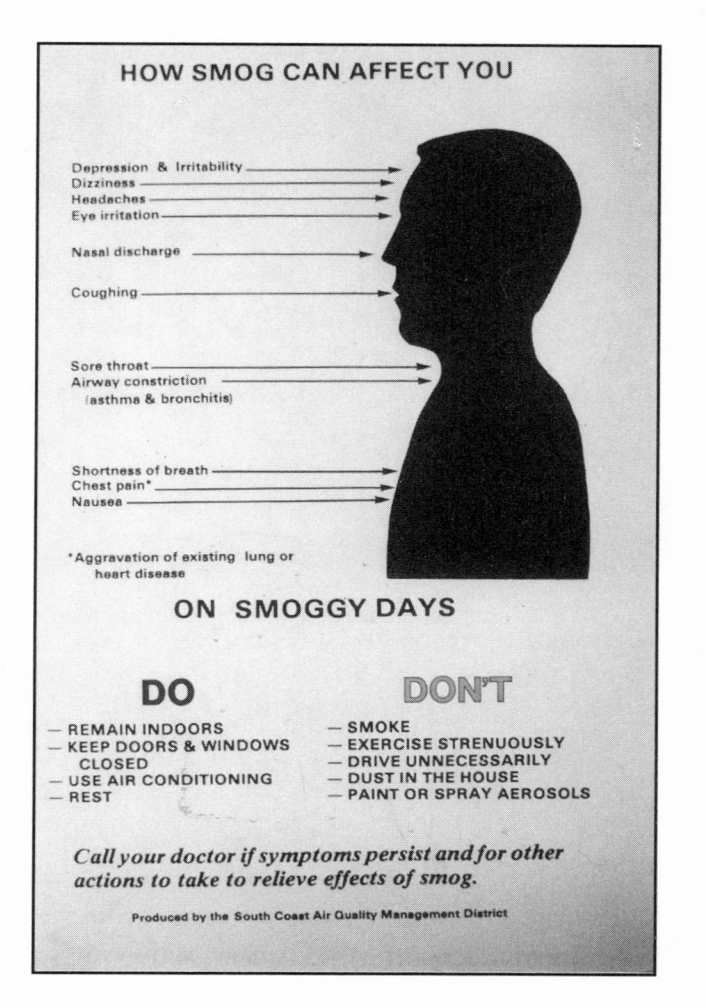

Smog is harmful to human health. CREDIT: *SOUTH COAST AIR QUALITY MANAGEMENT DISTRICT*

are still issued on a regular basis from May through October. The EPA considers the air unhealthy if it contains more than 0.12 parts per million of ozone in any given hour. Ozone levels in Los Angeles often reach three times the federal health standard and cause headaches, nausea, irritated nasal passages, and coughing. Especially susceptible are children, the elderly, athletes, and people with long-term illnesses such as asthma and heart disease.

Other U.S. cities such as Houston, New York, San Diego, Boston, Albuquerque, St. Louis, Chicago, Atlanta, and Washington, D.C., are also unable to meet federal ozone limits 365 days of the year. Air pollution should lessen, though, as new car models are developed. New cars have much better fuel economy than older models. This means that the car's engine makes better use of the gasoline, so it can travel farther for each gallon of gasoline used. Cars driven in the United States are required to have many pollution control devices. One of these is called a catalytic converter. It dramatically reduces hydrocarbon emissions.

By 1990 cars sold in California produced 90 percent fewer pollutants than automobiles manufactured in 1970. Also, a corporation established a "cash for clunkers" program. It paid about $700 each for cars manufactured before 1971. The purpose of the program was to get the old, polluting "clunkers" off the road by sending them to the scrap heap. But the air is still dirty because overall the number of cars has increased and they travel greater distances. In the 1950s many Americans changed the way they lived, moving from cities to suburbs. Commuting to work became a way of life for many people, making them dependent on the private car. This fact, along with increasing population, caused sales of automobiles to skyrocket, and miles and miles of highways were constructed. As the population, the number of cars, and the distances traveled all increased, so did city air pollution.

Unfortunately, pollutants produced in cities are sometimes carried to faraway places. Acadia National Park, located on a remote, heavily forested island off the Maine coast, has recorded ground-level ozone levels as high as those in Los Angeles. The ozone there results from the burning of fossil fuels in electric power plants, factories, and cars hundreds of miles away. When winds blow out of the southwest, they move pollutants collected in cities on the northeast coast, including Washington, D.C., Philadelphia, New York City, and Boston, to Acadia. Occasionally ozone levels are so high in the late spring and summer that visitors must be cautioned against taking long hikes on the lovely trails. When people exercise they breathe faster and inhale a greater volume of air. When the air is impure, a person's body is exposed to more pollutants.

The Pollutant Standards Index (PSI) is used to report the purity of the air. It translates measurements of the many pollutants in a specific area to a single number. When the PSI is greater than 100, the air is considered unhealthy. Reports are often included in local newspapers or on television and radio weather reports. You also can get information on air quality by calling your local American Lung Association.

PSI CATEGORIES AND HEALTH EFFECT DESCRIPTOR WORDS*

Index Range	Descriptor Words
0 to 50	Good
51 to 100	Moderate
101 to 199	Unhealthful
200 to 299	Very Unhealthful
300 and above	Hazardous

Taken from EPA-450/4-91-023, November 1991.

The United States is not alone in its air pollution problems. Prosperous Mexicans, like Americans, take pride in owning cars. However, until 1990 pollution controls in that country were either nonexistent or not enforced. Mexico City, the capital of Mexico and one of the world's largest cities, with a population of 15.3 million, is the smog capital of the world. Because Mexico City is located in the Valley of Mexico and surrounded by mountains, its pollutants become trapped by temperature inversions similar to the inversions in Los Angeles. In 1990 Mexico City failed to meet the World Health Organization's standards for clean air 310 days out of the year. Pollutants are spewed into the air from thousands of industries and from the tailpipes of millions of cars. Also contributing to the brew of air pollutants is leakage of bottled gas that millions of Mexicans use for cooking and heating. The fuel is stored in rooftop canisters. Scientists believe hydrocarbons escape into the atmosphere when the bottled gas is burned in stoves and heaters and when the canisters are refilled. To filter out particles in the choking air, some cyclists wear surgical masks.

Mexico City is 7,200 feet above sea level. This high altitude means that Mexico City has about one-third as much oxygen as there would be at sea level. In 1991 little booths called *casieta de oxygienia* were erected on some Mexico City streets. For a little under two dollars people could enter and breathe clean air for a minute.

Mexico's rapid industrialization, which has helped the country's economy, has come at a great environmental cost. This beautiful nation of mountains and deserts, rain forests and sandy coasts is starting to manage its pollution problems. Although it is being phased out, many of Mexico's older cars still burn gasoline that contains lead. Lead is added to improve engine performance, but as the gasoline is burned, it pollutes the air with poisonous lead compounds. Catalytic converters have been added to Mexico City's buses, and beginning in 1991 they were required on all new cars. The average city car is eleven years old, however, and strictly enforced emission control programs are needed. The *Hoy no Circula* (Day Without a Car) regulation requires that drivers find other means of transportation one day a week.

Motor vehicles are not the only source of air pollution. In Eastern Europe (eastern Germany, Poland, Czechoslovakia, Hungary, Romania, and Bulgaria) factories and electric generating plants are the major source. Under communist rule industries in these countries were developed rapidly with little regard for the environment. In 1989, when communism fell and these areas became more open, extensive pollution was found. In Romania, old factories emitted thousands of tons of soot into the air yearly, covering everything with a layer of grime. In some cities, a thick yellow-brown fog forced drivers to use their headlights even in daylight hours. This was due to the burning of soft, high-sulfur brown coal for heating and industry.

All fossil fuels contain sulfur (S), a pale yellow, nonmetallic **element**. An element is one of the more than one hundred basic materials out of which all other things are made. When coal, oil, and natural gas burn, the sulfur combines with oxygen to form sulfur dioxide (SO_2). Coal, the major contributor of sulfur dioxide, contains differing amounts of sulfur. Low-sulfur coal contains less than 1 percent. However, it costs more and produces less heat than the more polluting medium- and high-sulfur coals, which may contain as much as 5 percent.

The pollutants released when fossil fuels are burned include nitrogen oxides and small quantities of sulfur dioxide. In the atmosphere, these pollutants mix with water and oxygen in the presence of sunlight and form sulfuric and nitric acids. Eventually these acids return to the Earth in what is commonly called acid rain. Actually, the acids become part of snow, fog, and hail as well as rain. Sometimes they even form tiny dry acidic particles in dust or soot.

Sulfur dioxide and nitrogen oxide emissions from coal-burning electric power plants and motor vehicles are the primary causes of acid rain. To keep ground-level air cleaner, utilities and factories in the United States and Canada built higher and higher smokestacks. These "tall stacks" improve air quality in the surrounding area. However, they deposit pollutants higher into the atmosphere where they can be carried by the wind for thousands of miles.

Much of acid rain in the northeastern United States comes from sulfur dioxides and nitrogen oxides produced by power plants in the Ohio River Valley (comprising parts of Ohio, Illinois, Indiana, Kentucky, West Virginia, and Pennsylvania). Pollutants travel on the jet stream, a wind system in the upper troposphere that blows from west to east. If you have flown round-trip from coast to coast in the United States you know that it takes less time to fly eastward. This is because the wind in the jet stream pushes the plane along. Pollutants in the upper troposphere travel in the jet stream from the

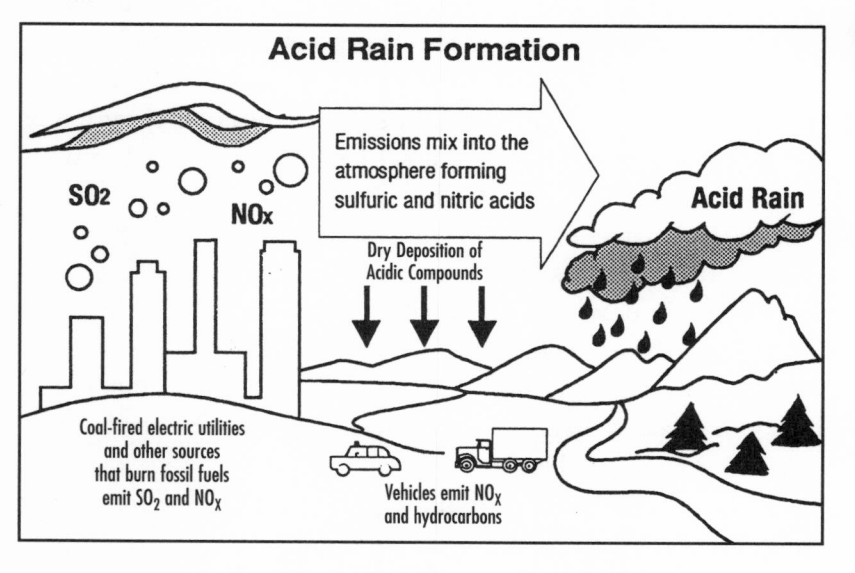

Acid Rain Formation

SO_2

NO_x

Emissions mix into the atmosphere forming sulfuric and nitric acids

Acid Rain

Dry Deposition of Acidic Compounds

Coal-fired electric utilities and other sources that burn fossil fuels emit SO_2 and NO_x

Vehicles emit NO_x and hydrocarbons

Sulfur dioxide and nitrogen oxide emissions react with water vapor and oxidants in the atmosphere and are chemically transformed into acidic compounds. These compounds are deposited in rain or snow; the compounds also join airborne particles and fall to Earth as dry deposition. CREDIT: U.S. ENVIRONMENTAL PROTECTION AGENCY industrial Midwest to the Northeast. The damage caused by these air pollutants shows how closely the atmosphere and the **biosphere** are linked. The biosphere is the portion of the Earth a few miles above and below sea level where all living things dwell.

Everything in the biosphere is part of an **ecosystem**. An ecosystem is a system of relationships that exists between living and nonliving things. Altering one element of an ecosystem affects many other parts of it. Acid rain can severely harm plants and animals. Some lakes have no fish, and evergreen trees are bare of needles in some forests throughout the world. But to understand how acid rain affects living things, first you must be familiar with acids, **bases**, and the pH scale, which is a measure of acidity.

Acids are sour and you are already familiar with many of them. If you ate a grapefruit for breakfast, the tangy taste was caused by citric acid. Acids are also present in many other fruits such as lemons, apples, pears, and tomatoes. Often you have put an acid on your salad, because vinegar, a common ingredient in salad dressing, is also an acid. Your stomach produces hydrochloric acid to help your body digest food. Automobile batteries contain sulfuric acid, an acid so strong it can cause burns. Bases are the chemical opposites of acids. They feel slippery and those that are edible have a bitter taste. Egg whites, baking soda, soap, and bleach are bases. Household ammonia, used for some household cleaning, is a poisonous base. When bases are dissolved in water, they form solutions called **alkalies**.

You can determine whether a liquid is an acid or a base by using an indicator. The indicator will change color when it is mixed into an acid or alkali solution. You can make your own indicator using a red cabbage.

Cut the cabbage into several large pieces and put them into a stainless steel or enamel pan. Cover the cabbage pieces with water, place the pan on the stove, and simmer over low heat for about one-half hour. Remove the pan from the stove and allow it to cool. The purplish liquid in the pan will be your indicator. Pour about one-half cup of it into each of two containers. To one container, add a teaspoon of baking soda. To the other, add a teaspoon of vinegar. Stir each solution with a clean spoon.

You should find that the baking soda solution turns the indicator blue, showing that it is a base. The vinegar, an acid, turns the indicator red. You can use the indicator to test various things in your house. Try testing lemon juice, cola, tomato juice, and laundry detergent. Can you tell if these liquids are acids or bases? Some liquids you try may have little effect on the purplish color of the indicator. These substances are neither acids nor bases; they are neutral.

The cabbage indicator can tell you whether something is an acid or a base, but it cannot tell you how acidic or alkaline

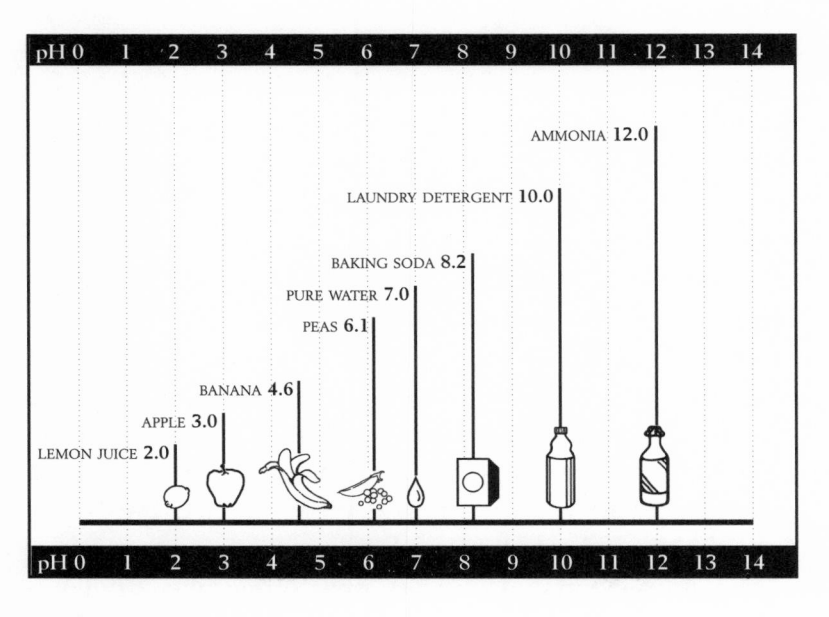

The pH of familiar things.

it is. Scientists use a pH scale to express these precise measurements. The scale ranges from 0 to 14. A number below 7 indicates that a solution is acidic, and a number above 7 indicates that a solution is alkaline. A neutral solution has a pH of 7.

The pH scale is logarithmic, meaning that a measurement of a pH 4 indicates that a solution is ten times more acidic than one with a pH 5, and one hundred times more acidic than pH 6. Indicator papers are used to tell the approximate pH of a substance. Ask your science teacher where you can purchase indicator, or litmus, paper. When you dip a strip of the paper into a solution it turns shades of red or blue indicating that it is an acid (red) or base (blue). If you are using indicator paper, you can compare the color of the paper to the color chart provided so you can determine the approximate pH of a substance.

You cannot tell by looking at or feeling rain whether it is normal rain or acid rain. But you can find out the approximate acidity of rain or snow if you have indicator paper. Place a clean container outdoors to collect precipitation and test your sample with the indicator paper. Ordinary rain is slightly acidic with a pH of less than 5.6. In the Great Plains unpolluted rain may have a pH as high as 6 or 7. But if your sample has a pH lower than 5.0, it is acid rain. The pH of the rain that falls in the Adirondack Mountains region of upper New York State averages around 4.2!

Typically, healthy clear-water lakes have a pH of 6.0 to 8.0. When acid rain falls on lakes and streams, their waters can in turn become acidic. According to the EPA, nearly 2,000 lakes and streams in parts of New Jersey, Delaware, Pennsylvania, Maryland, Virginia, West Virginia, and North Carolina are acidic due primarily to acid rain or snow.

Sometimes "acid shock" occurs in the spring when a buildup of acid rain pollutants is released into a body of water from rapidly melting snow. Just as you tested the pH of rainfall, you can collect a sample of water from a lake or stream near where you live and determine the pH. Do this regularly and record the results. Are the pH values constant, or do they change?

Some lakes have such acidic water that they no longer function normally. The water looks crystal clear, but that is because many of the plants and animals that naturally inhabit the lakes can no longer live there. **Algae**, a large group of water plants that have no roots or flowers, normally float in the water of healthy lakes. Their presence makes the water unclear. In acidified lakes these algae cannot survive.

In healthy clear-water lakes, bacteria and fungi break down dead plants and animals. The nutrients contained in their remains are released back into the soil and water, and are taken up by living things and used by them to grow. In acidified lakes this recycling of nutrients is interrupted. Layer upon layer of dead material builds up, forming thick mats on the lake bottom. Living things in the body of water can no longer survive.

29

Not all lakes and streams that are exposed to acid rain become acidic. This is due to substances called **buffers** that neutralize acids. When the rock surrounding a lake is limestone, as is the case around the Great Lakes, the soil is rich in calcium and magnesium, which act as buffers and neutralize the acids. You can observe buffering action by doing the following experiment.

Put about one-half cup of water in a glass measuring cup. Imagine that this is a small pond and test the pH with your indicator paper. Now, pretending that acid rain is falling on the pond, add one-fourth teaspoon of vinegar to the water. When you test the pH, you will find that it is much lower. Now add two antacid tablets that contain calcium carbonate, such as Tums or Alka-Seltzer, and stir until the tablets are dissolved. The tablets act like a buffer. When you test the pH again, you will find that it has risen because the antacid tablet has neutralized the acid. If you were to add more vinegar, and continue to test the pH, you would find that it dropped, because the buffering capacity of the antacid was being depleted.

This buffering depletion is exactly what happens in many Adirondack and New England lakes. They are surrounded by rocks that are covered by a thin layer of soil. The soil has little buffering capacity, and as acid rain continues to fall, the natural buffers are quickly used up and the water in the lakes becomes increasingly acidic. However, not all acidic waters are acidic because of acid rain. Many kinds of bogs and cedar swamps, for example, are naturally acidic. They have wet, spongy ground made up mostly of decayed plants, and often brown, foamy scum laps at the shore.

Changes in the number and kinds of living things in lakes and streams give clues that the acidity of a body of water may be increasing. Fewer fish and the disappearance of young fish, which are more sensitive to acid waters, might be a sign of trouble. Depending on the species, fish can tolerate varying levels of acidity. Northern pike, yellow perch, smallmouth bass, and lake trout die off when the water's pH is between 5.5 and 4.5. Most fish will die when the pH of their watery homes is lower than 4.5.

Acid rain harms fish in several ways. It upsets the salt balance in the fish's blood and causes its bones to lose calcium. This weakens the fish's skeleton, which becomes twisted and deformed, interfering with the fish's ability to swim. In the female, calcium is also essential for the production of eggs. Secondly, some metals that are poisonous to fish that are a normal part of the soil are dissolved out by acid water. Even a very small amount of one of these, aluminum, is toxic to fish. Aluminum collects on the gills and, as a protective response, the fish's body produces mucus. Soon the mucus becomes so thick it coats the gills and they appear white.

They become clogged, and the fish suffocates. Large fish are less affected by acid water directly. However, they may be unsafe for humans to eat if caught in acid waters because of high concentrations of another poisonous metal, mercury, in their meat.

Acid rain affects **invertebrates** (animals without backbones) as well. It dissolves the shells of clams, crayfish, freshwater mussels, shrimp, and snails. Salamanders breed and deposit their eggs in small ponds. In some areas spring thaws result in acid shock in these small bodies of water. When the eggs hatch and young salamanders live in water that has a pH of 5.0 or less, they may not develop normally. In the same way, the infertility of some frog eggs and deformities in tadpoles can be blamed on acid rain.

Invertebrates that live in soil as well as water are affected by acid rain. Earthworms are nature's great recyclers, feeding on decaying leaves, grasses, and insects, and releasing the nutrients back into the soil. However, if the pH of the soil drops to 4.0, earthworms can no longer function normally.

The effects of acid rain are felt by the mighty red spruce and balsam firs on some mountain slopes as well as by tiny earthworms. Scientists studied Camel's Hump, a 4,100-foot peak in Vermont's Green Mountains, which is often covered with acid deposition in the form of fog and mist. They found that the acids damage evergreen needles by wearing away the protective waxy coating. Gradually, little brown spots appear on the needles' surface and cause them to drop off. Dieback is the name for this process that begins at the treetops and branch tips and spreads downward and inward. This weakens the tree, making it more susceptible to insects and harsh weather conditions. Trees such as sugar maples, white birch, and beech that grow at lower elevations grow more slowly in the presence of acid rain. Where once lush green forests grew, patches of barren trees now dot the landscape.

AIR ALERT

Air pollutants (sulfur dioxide, nitrogen oxides, and ozone) and acid rain are thought to be major causes of forest decline worldwide. CREDIT: MARK G. TJOELKER

In addition to affecting lakes, streams, and forests, acid rain **corrodes** metals and causes stone and paint to deteriorate. From the Parthenon in Greece, to Europe's magnificent cathedrals, to the Lincoln Memorial in Washington, D.C., surfaces are **eroding** and gradually crumbling. Just as acid rain frees poisonous metals in soil, it may cause the lead in solder that is used to hold pipes together as well as the copper in the pipes to dissolve in drinking water. These dissolved metals make the water impure.

In the 1960s many people in the United States became concerned about the quality of the air. In 1970, the U.S. Congress passed the Clean Air Act. This law has been amended to reflect ongoing concerns and problems with air quality. The law established "National Ambient Air Quality Standards" (NAAQS) to specify the maximum amount of six

The nitric and sulfuric acids that produce acid rain have eroded the stone and blurred the details of this statue. CREDIT: ARTHUR BEALE

pollutants that can be released into the air. The six regulated pollutants are sulfur dioxide, nitrogen oxides, carbon monoxide, lead, ozone, and particulate matter. These are considered to be harmful to public health.

Because of these laws, the air in American cities is becoming much cleaner. Between 1970 and 1990 the amount of lead discharged into the atmosphere from battery factories, smelters, refineries, and other sources decreased 97 percent. Particulates, dust, and grime in the air have decreased 59 percent in the same period.

Clean Air Act amendments of 1990 and 1992 allow companies to buy and sell pollution rights. For example, a company that releases more than the allowable amount of pollutants into the air may buy pollution credits from a company that controls pollution beyond required limits. Or the company might install equipment that reduces pollutants released into the air. Even an ambitious van-pooling program that would save lots of individual car trips to and from the company can help a company meet air purity standards. This arrangement of buying and selling pollution credits means that polluters have to pay for the damage they are doing to the atmosphere.

Federal environmental laws such as the Clean Air Act are enforced by the EPA. The EPA was established as a federal agency soon after the first celebration of Earth Day in 1970. It has the authority to impose fines and criminal penalties on those who break environmental laws. This agency evaluates the purity of the nation's air in two ways. One is by directly measuring the concentrations of pollutants in the air. This is done at the more than 4,000 monitoring stations around the country. Sensitive instruments analyze the **ambient**, or surrounding, air and the results are sent to the EPA. The second method for determining air quality is to calculate emissions. This means devising an estimate of pollutants released into the air every year based on engineering studies. Using this information the EPA can identify problem areas.

Under the Clean Air Act state governments are responsible for meeting the NAAQS. Most factories with tall smokestacks are required to have devices that measure pollutants coming out of them. Each state must submit a plan to the EPA for approval detailing what action it will take to

Environmental Protection Specialist Molly Magoon inspects a vehicle's emission control devices. CREDIT: R. BRUCE MCKAY

address air pollution. For example, individual power plants can reduce sulfur dioxide emissions by switching to low-sulfur coal, installing scrubber equipment that removes acid rain pollutants from chimney smoke, and by producing electricity with furnaces that burn cleaner and more efficiently. Under the Clean Air Act amendments, the Acid Rain Program requires huge reductions in nitrogen oxide emissions and also sulfur dioxide from electric utilities.

The EPA has many employees who work to enforce the regulations of the Clean Air Act. Molly Magoon is one of the professionals who works in this capacity. She writes: "I grew up in Ann Arbor, Michigan, and hold a Bachelor of Arts degree from the University of Michigan. When I joined the EPA nine years ago, I worked in the legal department. There I was introduced to the interesting and important work of this agency.

"In my current position, my official title is 'Environmental Protection Specialist.' My job is interesting, rewarding, and at times exciting. I describe myself as an 'environmental police officer' because I carry 'credentials.' These look like a badge and identify and authorize me to inspect auto repair shops. (There are EPA criminal investigators, called 'Special Agents,' who carry guns, but I do not.)

"My job is to make sure that auto repair shop facilities such as service stations and muffler shops do not remove emission control devices, such as catalytic converters, air pumps, and exhaust gas recirculation valves. These devices reduce the amount of air pollution that is emitted into the air from automobiles and trucks. I also enforce new laws and regulations that control the use of ozone-depleting coolant in automotive air conditioners. Repair shops are required to recycle the coolant so that it does not damage the atmosphere. Other inspectors for EPA inspect many other sources of pollution such as smokestacks, chemicals at factories, pesticides, sewage treatment plants, oil refineries, and even cranberry juice factories, to name a few.

"I recently served a search warrant with an EPA attorney and two armed United States Marshals. We needed a search warrant because the owner of a service station would not cooperate with the EPA. By enforcing regulations under the Clean Air Act I help to protect our air and the environment."

Keeping cars in good working order is important in reducing air pollution. In areas of the United States that cannot meet Clean Air Act standards, motor vehicle inspection and maintenance programs are required by law. These help to reduce nitrogen oxide, carbon monoxide, and hydrocarbon emissions. Newer emission tests analyze exhaust gases from the tailpipe as the car is driven on a treadmill-like device so as to test whether fuel vapor is properly burned. The car's system is also checked for leaks that allow fuel vapors to escape into the atmosphere. Standards for passing the inspection are determined by a vehicle's age. This is because as new car models are designed, they are required to meet stricter pollution control standards. Vehicles fifteen years old or less that do not pass emission tests when they are inspected cannot be registered until they have been repaired. If the repairs are more than $450, the EPA may allow the motor vehicle to be operated temporarily.

Pollutants that cause acid rain travel on the wind from cities to rural areas and across national boundaries. We are constantly reminded of the presence of pollution whether we ride bikes on city streets, hear air-quality reports on television, or are unable to see the beauty of distant mountain ranges. People are concerned about their own health, as well as the well-being of the millions of other species that live on Earth and depend on clean air and pure water.

CHAPTER THREE

EARTH'S CHANGING CLIMATE— THE POWER OF GREENHOUSE GASES

The terms "greenhouse effect" and "global warming" are often used interchangeably in newspaper articles, magazines, and on broadcast news. However, they have different meanings. The greenhouse effect is the natural process by which certain gases in the atmosphere keep the Earth considerably warmer than an airless planet would be. This process has existed throughout time. Without the greenhouse effect, our planet would be covered with snow and ice and the average temperature would be zero.

You can feel the greenhouse effect yourself. On a clear, dry evening out-of-doors, you will feel the temperature drop as soon as the sun goes down. On a humid or cloudy evening you won't notice much temperature change at sundown because the clouds and water vapor in the atmosphere are radiating the heat down at you.

Now scientists are becoming concerned because the concentration of greenhouse gases in the atmosphere is increasing. Global warming usually refers to the concern that recent human-made increases in greenhouse gases will make the greenhouse effect stronger and thus make Earth warmer.

The Earth's ability to trap heat through the greenhouse effect is balanced by the Earth's capacity to reflect heat. This keeps the Earth's average temperature at 59 degrees. The whiteness of ice and snow reflects more heat than the darker sea and land. The vast **ice sheets** in the Arctic and Antarctica, remnants of the last **ice age**, are prime reflectors of solar energy. The Antarctic ice sheet at the South Pole is the largest on Earth. It is about one and a half times as big as the continental United States and is 2.5 miles thick in some places! Because of the severe cold in Antarctica (the average air temperature remains below zero degrees) snow and ice rarely melt. At the North Pole, the Arctic includes the Arctic Ocean, Greenland, Alaska, Siberia, northern Canada, Scandinavia, and Iceland. Almost all of Greenland, which is about three times the size of Texas, is covered with ice throughout the year.

Throughout Earth's history, climate has changed slowly over thousands of years. An increased greenhouse effect may have contributed to the "Mesozoic hothouse" (or global warming) that existed 100 million years ago, during the age of dinosaurs. At that time many parts of the Earth are thought to have been considerably warmer than they are today. Natural variations in the temperature of the Earth like this lead to uncertainties about the theory of global warming.

The so-called greenhouse gases are better heat absorbers than other gases. Are we tinkering with Earth's climate by increasing the amounts of greenhouse gases in the atmosphere? Have human beings become as powerful as the forces of nature? Are we conducting an unintended experiment in the atmosphere that could affect all life on Earth?

The climate of an area is determined in part by a region's **latitude**. Parallels of latitude are imaginary lines that run east and west around the Earth. They measure distance in degrees north and south from the Equator (0 degrees) to the North and South Poles (90 degrees). How close a place is to the equator generally determines how hot or cold it is.

Climates can be grouped into zones. The equator divides the globe into two equal parts called the Northern Hemisphere and the Southern Hemisphere. The tropical zone extends north and south from the equator. In the Northern Hemisphere, it ends at the parallel of latitude called the Tropic of Cancer. In the Southern Hemisphere it ends at the parallel of latitude called the Tropic of Capricorn. The United States is located in the temperate zone. In the Northern Hemisphere, it is the area between the Tropic of Cancer and the Arctic Circle. In the Southern Hemisphere the temperate zone is between the Tropic of Capricorn and the Antarctic Circle. The polar regions lie above the temperate zone in the Northern Hemisphere and below it in the Southern Hemisphere.

The climate within these zones is predictable for several reasons. The atmosphere surrounding our planet is in continuous motion. This motion is caused by the rotation of the Earth and the fact that the sun heats our planet unevenly. The warmest area of the planet is the tropical zone. The sun heats the air in this hot, humid area. It becomes lighter and rises. This moisture-laden air moves toward the poles, becoming cooler and bringing rain and snow to other parts of the planet. Cooler air rushes toward the equator to take its place.

The atmosphere has an important partner in regulating the world's climate. It is the oceans that cover more than 70 percent of our planet. Where the surface layer of the ocean and the atmosphere meet, there is an exchange of heat. The top 10 feet of the ocean water is capable of storing more heat than the entire atmosphere. Some of this absorbed heat warms the uppermost layers of the ocean waters and some of

The oceans and atmosphere are partners in regulating the Earth's climate.
CREDIT: SCOTT N. MILLER

it is mixed into the depths. Water warms and cools more slowly than air or land. In the hot summer months, the oceans absorb and store heat that warms coastal areas during the winter. Conversely, it is pleasant to visit ocean beaches during the summer months because the cooler seawater absorbs heat from the air to make the air cooler.

Like the air in the atmosphere, the water in oceans also moves in predictable patterns. **Currents** move through the oceans like rivers of saltwater. The Gulf Stream, for example, is a huge ocean current that originates in the Caribbean Sea near the equator. It travels into the Gulf of Mexico, around the tip of Florida and north along the East Coast. Much of the water travels all the way to Newfoundland. The water in the Gulf Stream is 11 to 18 degrees warmer than the surrounding water. Air that blows across the Gulf Stream becomes warmer. The winter climate in England and Norway is warmer than other climates of the same latitude because air warmed by the Gulf Stream blows over these countries.

The 1980s was the hottest decade since weather records were kept, beginning 130 years ago. In the summer of 1988 New England sweltered under a heat wave, the Midwest suffered from a severe drought, and soil in parched Texas fields resembled sand. Some people feared that predictions of global warming were coming true and others felt the heat and drought were coincidental. Some studies seemed to attribute global warming and cooling to sun spots. These are dark patches on the sun's surface that appear and disappear in regular cycles. The only certainty that remained at the end of the decade was the controversy that surrounds global warming.

The Earth has complicated and rapidly changing weather and only a small number of reliable weather observations have been collected over time. The best estimates indicate that temperatures have increased about one degree since the Industrial Revolution began. Climate scientists debate whether the rise in global temperature over the past century is a natural variation or is caused by human activities.

The Mauna Loa climate observatory in Hawaii has been measuring carbon dioxide in the atmosphere since 1958. There, the air is clean after having traveled over thousands of miles of sea, far away from sources of pollution. Unless the observatory's neighboring volcano is active, there is little to make the air dirty. The findings at Mauna Loa indicate that the amount of carbon dioxide in the atmosphere rises steadily every year. Generally, scientists believe that if this continues, by the middle of the twenty-first century Earth's temperature will be approximately 2 to 6 degrees warmer than it is today.

You probably remember that carbon dioxide is exhaled by animals as they breathe and used by plants in photosynthesis. It is also produced when coal, oil, gas, or wood is burned to produce energy. Because we are burning more of these fuels than ever before, we are releasing huge amounts of carbon stored in them. This carbon combines with oxygen, increasing the amount of carbon dioxide in our atmosphere. According to a report by the United Nations Environmental Programme, the amount of carbon dioxide in the atmosphere may double by the year 2050. This could cause the temperature of the Earth to rise.

Carbon dioxide is an important trace gas. It is a gas that you can't smell, taste, or see. If you blow out through a straw into a glass of water, the bubbles are mostly carbon dioxide. You also see evidence of its existence every time you open a can or bottle of soda. The bubbles that are in your carbonated drink are carbon dioxide.

Carbon dioxide is a combination of two different elements, carbon (C) and oxygen (O). For each part of carbon, there are two parts of oxygen. You already know that oxygen is essential for animals to breathe. Carbon is also very important in the cycle of life on Earth. In fact the element carbon is part of every living or once-living thing. Carbon has many forms, and you have surely seen some types of it. In its hardest form, it is a sparkling diamond, and in its softest form it is graphite, one of the ingredients in the marking material in your pencil. If you have ever burned bread while toasting it, the black that you see is carbon. The charcoal that you use for grilling food outside is also mostly carbon.

Carbon combines not only with oxygen, but with many other elements as it circulates through the biosphere. To understand what is called the carbon cycle, think of a blueberry bush. Like all plants, it needs carbon dioxide to survive. It gives off much of the oxygen it takes in, but the carbon becomes part of the plant. The carbon is used to make the plant grow and becomes part of the blueberries, the fruit the plant produces. Now imagine that a hungry bird swoops down and eats some of the berries. The bird stores some of the carbon from the berries in its body, and the carbon helps its body grow. Some carbon returns to the Earth in the bird's droppings. The bird exhales some of the carbon in the form of carbon dioxide. Finally, carbon dioxide is released when the bird dies and its body decays. In these ways carbon dioxide rejoins the Earth and the atmosphere and is available to start the cycle again.

Another important part of the carbon cycle involves the constant exchange between carbon dioxide in the atmosphere and the oceans. Carbon dioxide dissolves in ocean water, and **phytoplankton**, sea plants so tiny they can only be seen with a microscope, use it to make food, just as plants on land do. When the plants remove the carbon dioxide dissolved in seawater, the sea is able to absorb more from the atmosphere. **Marine** animals and fish eat the plants and store carbon in their bodies just as the bird did. When they die, they are either eaten, passing the carbon on to other marine life, or their bodies sink to the bottom of the sea, making the sea floor a natural carbon storage place. Some of the carbon dissolves in seawater to form carbonates of which **coral** and the shells of many small sea creatures are made. Oceans contain more than fifty times the amount of carbon found in the atmosphere. The oceans' ability to store carbon dioxide greatly reduces the amount of this gas in the atmosphere, which is important in stabilizing the Earth's temperature.

The world's climate scientists believe the present increase in carbon dioxide and other greenhouse gases is caused by human activities. These experts study ancient climates so that they will be better able to predict what will happen in the future. One way they do this is by studying the ice in Greenland and Antarctica. These areas are so cold that they are covered with ice and snow that never melt. The new snow that falls each year forms a distinct layer on top of that already on the ground. The under layers pressed down by snow on top of them turn to ice. You have probably seen this happen if you have made a snowball. As you shape and enlarge it, the snowball becomes icy. In Antarctica so much icy snow forms that it grows into ice sheets that can be several miles thick. As each layer forms, tiny bubbles of air are sealed inside.

Scientists, working outside in freezing conditions, drill deep into ice caps to obtain samples called ice cores. In the summer of 1993, they drilled through two miles of ice. After transporting the cores to laboratories, they work in room-size freezers to analyze them. By studying the ice layers in the

Scientists drill into ice caps to obtain samples called ice cores. CREDIT: NATIONAL SCIENCE FOUNDATION

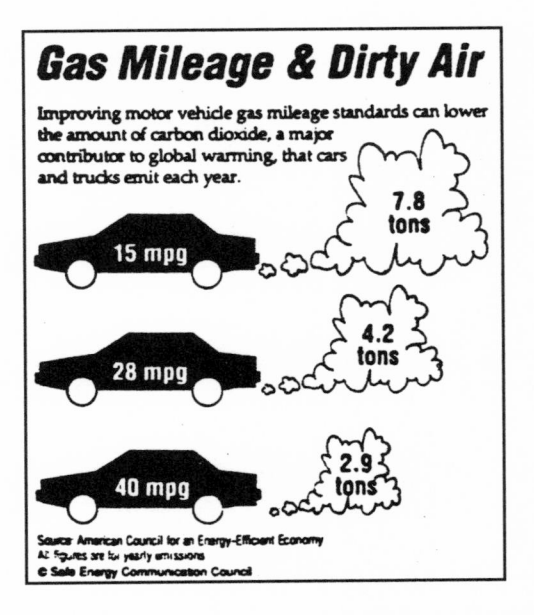

Gas Mileage & Dirty Air

Improving motor vehicle gas mileage standards can lower the amount of carbon dioxide, a major contributor to global warming, that cars and trucks emit each year.

15 mpg — 7.8 tons

28 mpg — 4.2 tons

40 mpg — 2.9 tons

Source: American Council for an Energy-Efficient Economy
All figures are for yearly emissions
© Safe Energy Communication Council

Improved gas mileage reduces the amount of pollutants that a vehicle emits.
CREDIT: AMERICAN COUNCIL FOR AN ENERGY-EFFICIENT ECONOMY AND THE SAFE ENERGY COMMUNICATION COUNCIL

cores, they can identify single years of climate as long ago as 250,000 years. They crush parts of the cores and analyze the trapped air bubbles they contain. Researchers have learned that the composition of gases in the atmosphere has varied throughout time. By studying ice core gases, scientists have learned that levels of carbon dioxide are the biggest factor in climate change. As carbon dioxide levels dropped, temperatures became cooler.

There are other greenhouse gases that are more powerful heat trappers than carbon dioxide. Methane is a gas that comes from a variety of natural sources. It is released from rotting materials in garbage dumps and by tiny organisms that live in waterlogged soils such as marshes and the fields where rice is grown, called "rice paddies." Cattle, sheep, and even termites produce methane as their digestive tracts break down the plants they eat. Each **molecule**, or particle, of methane absorbs twenty to thirty times as much heat as each carbon dioxide molecule. Because there is much less methane than carbon dioxide in the atmosphere, methane contributes only about 10 to 15 percent of the greenhouse effect.

Other powerful greenhouse gases are the chlorofluoro-carbons (CFCs). They are a combination of three elements— chlorine, fluorine, and carbon. CFCs do not occur naturally on Earth. They were developed in laboratories in the 1930s and manufactured for use in such things as air conditioners, refrigerators, insulation, and aerosol spray cans. CFCs are up to twenty thousand times more powerful than carbon dioxide in absorbing heat. They are responsible for 15 to 20 percent of the greenhouse effect. Nitrous oxide, another important greenhouse gas, contributes about 10 percent of the greenhouse effect. It is produced by automobile exhausts and is also released by nitrogen fertilizers that farmers use on their crops.

Those of us who live in the developed nations depend on coal, oil, and natural gas for much of our energy. In one year, we use fossil fuels that took about one million years to form. In so doing, we are polluting the air we breathe, using up fuels that are in limited supply, and disrupting and speeding up the natural carbon cycle.

Our lifestyle is dependent on cars, buses, trains, and planes to transport us from one place to another for both pleasure and business. We use products made from oil such as asphalt to pave our roads, and plastics for everything from toys to machinery. We grow our food on huge, sprawling farms using gasoline-powered tractors, combines, and planting machines. We burn fossil fuels in power plants to generate electricity that we use to operate lights, televisions, dishwashers, refrigerators, and business and manufacturing machinery. Most of our houses are heated by electricity, oil, or natural gas in the winter. If there is a power failure and we lose our electricity, our society grinds to a standstill.

Although these and other greenhouse gases compose a very tiny part of the atmosphere, they have a powerful effect. They trap heat energy from the sun that would normally escape into space after having warmed the Earth. As worldwide population increases, we will burn more fossil fuels, grow more rice, raise more cattle, and use more fertilizers on agricultural crops. All of these activities will add greenhouse gases to the atmosphere. Some of the gases remain in the atmosphere for long periods of time. Nitrous oxide can remain for more than a century, while CFCs can remain for fifty to five hundred years.

One reason scientists are concerned about rising temperatures is because of the possible melting of **glaciers** and ice sheets that could cause sea levels to rise. In Greenland and Antarctica, huge amounts of fresh water are contained in the vast ice sheets that cover the rocky land beneath. There is also lots of frozen water floating in the form of **icebergs**.

You can observe the effect of melting ice on water level by doing the following experiment. Put an ice cube in a glass and fill the glass to the brim with water, making sure that none spills over. If it does, wipe the outside dry. When the ice cube melts, the water will still be at the brim. This is because ice takes up more space than water. You can see by this experiment that melting icebergs would not contribute to rising sea levels. However, if the Earth became so warm that the ice sheets covering Greenland and Antarctica actually began to melt, the result would be like placing an ice cube on a solid surface like your kitchen counter. Vast amounts of icy water would run off the land into the sea. As the water warmed, it would expand, also contributing to rising sea levels.

The impact of rising sea levels would affect people around the world. Sea-level rise results in loss of land through erosion. This wearing away by the action of wind and waves, tides and currents carries the sand, rocks, mud, and soil out to

Like an ice cube in a glass of water, only the tip of an iceberg is visible. Seven-eighths of the iceberg is below the ocean's surface. CREDIT: NATIONAL SCIENCE FOUNDATION. PHOTO BY J. KATSUFRAKIS

sea. If you have ever built a sand castle on an ocean beach near the water you have probably seen it toppled with the incoming tide. If sea level rises, the entire beach on which you built your castle could be underwater, even at low tide.

Rising sea levels in populated areas could cause foundations of buildings to crumble, bridge supports to sink, highway pavement to buckle, and sewage treatment plants to be flooded with saltwater. Because of the importance of shipping, many of the world's cities are built on the seacoast. Flooding would occur in many of them, including New York, Miami, San Francisco, London, Buenos Aires, Venice, and Bangkok.

Rising sea levels would affect countries around the world. Egypt is mostly a land of desert. Its population is concentrated along the fertile Nile Valley. If rising sea levels caused

Higher tides caused by rising sea levels could be devastating to heavily built-up coastal areas. CREDIT: ANNE SMRCINA, MASSACHUSETTS COASTAL ZONE MANAGEMENT

flooding in this area, a large part of the nation's productive farmland would be lost and millions of people would be forced to leave their homes. If sea levels rose just 18 inches, one-third of the island of Jamaica and many small Pacific Islands would disappear.

Coastal swamps, salt marshes, and river deltas are low-lying areas that provide homes to millions of plants and animals. The invading sea would change the amount of salt in the water in these areas where clams, oysters, shrimp, and many other shellfish reproduce. Many species would not survive. Saltwater flooding these areas would prevent birds from resting and feeding there during their long migrations. Saltwater flooding would make supplies of freshwater unfit for people to drink.

Barrier beaches and barrier islands are ridges of sand that

rise slightly above the surface of the sea and run roughly parallel to the shore. They protect inland areas from storms. If
sea level rises, the barrier beaches and islands would be
underwater. This would be devastating to some barriers that
are heavily built up, such as Galveston Island, Texas; Ocean
City, Maryland; and Hilton Head, South Carolina. The tourist
industry in popular vacation places like Florida would suffer
greatly.

To build enough breakwaters, seawalls, jetties, and groins
to hold back the sea would cost billions of dollars. In the
Netherlands, which means "the low lands," about one-third of
the country lies below sea level. To keep back the water, in
1986 the Dutch completed an eight-billion-dollar system of
dams and dikes. Many poorer nations such as Bangladesh
could not afford such projects. Furthermore, many scientists
and engineers believe they would be ineffective against the
power of the sea in places such as barrier beaches and islands.
Businesses, farms, and houses near the sea could be destroyed,
leaving people homeless and without incomes or food.

As Arctic and Antarctic ice sheets shrink from the increase
in global temperatures, the heat that was once reflected back
into space from the glaring whiteness would be absorbed by
the seas and the flat, treeless plains called **tundra**. This could
cause further warming of the planet.

Global warming would also change climate and weather
patterns. Scientists believe that temperatures would rise
faster near the poles than near the equator and that tropical
areas would receive more rain, while mid-latitudes, such as
the American Midwest, would receive less rainfall. The
Southwestern desert could move north to the Midwest and
the Midwestern grain belt could shift north into Canada.
Farmers may have to plant different crops to accommodate
the new climate conditions. Northern lands that are now too
frozen to grow food may become suitable farm lands. If the

Earth warms, forests would gradually move away from the equator toward the cooler climates of the polar regions. This would affect the thousands of animals that inhabit the forests and force them to move as well.

Within any **biological** community there is an interdependency among the living things and the physical environment. Have you ever had an aquarium? In it, you put water, fish, plants, and sand or rocks. Given proper light and temperature conditions and a little food, this biological community can survive for a long time. However, if you give your aquarium too little light, the plants will not grow properly and will perhaps die. This may affect the fish that nibble on them for food. Or, if you slightly raise the water temperature, the fish may die. You can see how changes can affect the **biodiversity**, or variety of living things, in a small aquarium.

Coral polyps, the tiny marine animals that build coral reefs in tropical regions, may be some of the first victims if global warming occurs. Coral reefs normally live for hundreds of years but scientists are concerned that very warm water may be causing their death in Puerto Rico, Jamaica, the Cayman Islands, Haiti, Cuba, and the Florida Keys. Most coral animals live in shallow water where sunlight is intense and water temperature is close to the upper limit they can tolerate. They depend on tiny plants called coralline algae, a kind of seaweed, to grow and live.

Coralline algae produce limestone, a cementlike substance that forms the building blocks of coral reefs. When seawater temperature rises, the relationship between plants and animals of the coral reefs is disturbed. The coral colonies are deprived of vital nutrients and starve. The colorful coral polyps die, exposing the limestone. The coral reef, once an array of beautiful, exotic colors, looks like bleached stone.

In contrast to the warm tropics, polar regions are the world's refrigerators. Some experts, though, believe that

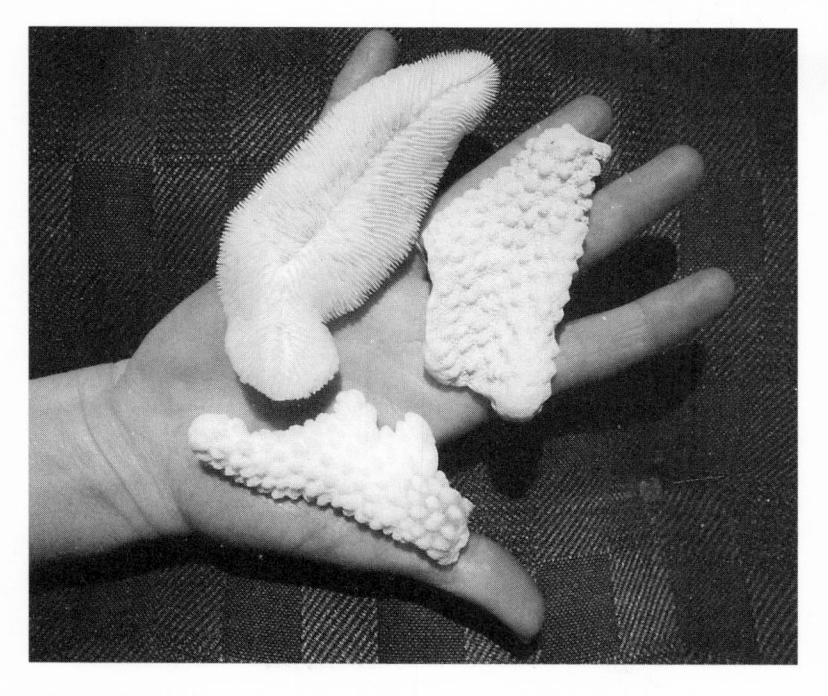

This coral island in the South Pacific is made up of the same corals as in the photo below. CREDITS: SCOTT N. MILLER

global warming will raise temperatures two to three times as much in the Arctic as in temperate zones in the next fifty to one hundred years. If temperatures increase, the biodiversity will be affected. Some species may adapt to warmer climates, but if the climate changes too quickly many will not be able to survive because they will be unable to find another suitable **habitat**. Destruction of habitat is the world's leading cause of loss of species today.

Climatic change is difficult to predict because the atmosphere is a very complex system. It is governed by the interactions among living things, oceans, air, snow and ice, dust, the sun, clouds, and other factors. Scientists are still learning how all of these pieces fit into the puzzle that results in our climate. To predict what the climate will be like in the future, scientists use computer models. They set up a "make-believe" Earth inside the computer, entering what they know about it. Once the model is built, the scientists can manipulate it to see what effect different inputs (such as increasing greenhouse gases) will have. This way they can try to predict what the climate will be like in the future. However, since much is still unknown about the atmosphere and its interactions, the models may not take into account all important factors. But they allow scientists to make an educated guess about what the future climate will be, based on what they know now.

Clouds both warm and cool the Earth. Made of water vapor and ice crystals, white clouds reflect some of the sun's rays back into space. In this way they act like window shades for the planet, cooling it. But clouds also absorb some of the heat radiated from the Earth, warming the atmosphere. Furthermore, if global warming occurs, more moisture would evaporate from the Earth's surface and more clouds would form. This is why one atmospheric scientist calls clouds "the wild cards" in computer modeling.

EARTH'S CHANGING CLIMATE

The difficulty in predicting future climate hinders experts in predicting what effect an increase in greenhouse gases will have. There is debate about what quantity of greenhouse gases will be emitted in the future and how they will concentrate in the atmosphere. However, most scientists would agree that life on Earth and the atmosphere coexist in a very delicate balance. Once the balance is upset, the consequences could be severe.

CHAPTER FOUR

PROTECTING STRATOSPHERIC OZONE— EARTH'S GLOBAL SUNSCREEN

Ozone, a pollutant when found in sufficient quantities at ground level, is a protector of all life on Earth when it is in the stratosphere. There it protects us from some of the sun's harsh ultraviolet rays. The ozone layer was discovered when balloon and rocket flights brought back information about a temperature change in the upper stratosphere. Because the ozone layer absorbs some of the sun's energy, it is much warmer than the layers of atmosphere on either side of it.

The distance of the ozone layer from the surface of the Earth and the amount of ozone it contains are not the same in all parts of the world. The ozone layer is closest to the Earth over the poles, where it extends from about 7 to 20 miles high. At the equator it is about 9 miles above the surface, extending up to 34 miles in the stratosphere. Because of the expanse of the ozone layer, you might think there is a lot of ozone in it. Actually, the amount of ozone is very small. At the atmospheric pressure of sea level, the ozone layer would be only as thick as the fabric in an umbrella.

Unlike the oxygen in the air we breathe, which is made up of two atoms of oxygen (O_2), ozone (O_3) has three atoms of oxygen. An **atom** is the smallest particle of a substance that contains all its characteristics. You may have smelled ozone if you live in an area where there are severe thunderstorms. It is the sharp, irritating odor that is often present after lightning has struck nearby. In fact, the word *ozone* comes from the German word *ozein*, which means "to smell."

Ozone in the stratosphere is produced when high energy sunlight strikes oxygen, splitting it apart. Then some of the free oxygen atoms combine with the regular oxygen to form ozone. The sun is strongest at the equator, and the highest levels of ozone production are in equatorial regions. Because of this you would expect the most ozone to be found there, too, but this is not the case. The amount of ozone over Minnesota is usually 30 percent greater than that over Texas, 900 miles farther south. Winds transport the ozone away from the equator, and the highest levels are found far away at the poles. Even during the long polar winters when darkness prevails for months and no ozone could be formed in polar areas, the largest total amount of ozone is still found at these latitudes. The destruction in the Antarctic ozone layer occurs and forms a hole for about two months when the return of sunlight marks the beginning of spring.

The ozone layer has been part of our atmosphere for at least a billion years, since the process of photosynthesis gradually built up an atmosphere containing oxygen. However, it was not something that was formed once and can never be made again. The ozone layer is replenished continuously. Until recently, the amount of ozone that was destroyed by natural processes was balanced by its natural formation.

The story of the destruction of the ozone layer begins in the 1930s when scientists discovered that the CFCs they developed in their laboratories could be used as refrigerants. Ice had been used to keep food cold for thousands of years. It was cut from lakes and ponds in the winter and stored in ice houses for use during the warm seasons. Older people in your community may remember when ice was delivered to their houses, sometimes by horse-drawn carriages. The heavy block of ice was put in an icebox where it kept food cool. As the ice melted, the water had to be emptied. The temperature in the icebox depended on how much ice was present.

In the 1920s mechanical refrigeration became available. Refrigerators were much more effective than iceboxes in preserving food by keeping it cold and at a constant temperature. In the early days of refrigeration **ammonia** was usually used as the coolant. This is a poisonous, sharp-smelling gas. It corroded the refrigerator coils and caused leaks to develop in them.

For this reason, the invention of refrigeration that used CFCs was considered a major advance. By the end of the 1930s a company named Du Pont was manufacturing Freon, a brand-name coolant. It was a liquid containing CFCs that soon would be used throughout the world for refrigeration and air-conditioning. CFCs seemed like a miracle chemical, because it was nonpoisonous and did not seem to react with anything. It did not appear to affect air or water or to harm any plants and animals. The manufacture of Freon increased, and it was used as a propellant in the aerosol spray cans for many products, including shaving cream, insecticides, hair sprays, and deodorants.

For over fifty years CFCs have been part of our daily lives and they have shaped the way we live. Because they were so readily available and reasonably priced, they made our lives more comfortable. We could ride in air-conditioned cars and shop in climate-controlled malls. CFCs were used in the manufacture of foam insulating material for buildings; packaging containers for meat, eggs, and fast foods; for foam in automobile seat cushions and carpet padding; and in chemicals for cleaning computer chips.

In the early 1970s, Dr. James Lovelock, later the proponent of the Gaia theory, became interested in measuring CFCs in the atmosphere. He proposed that all the CFCs that had ever been manufactured would still be in the atmosphere because they were very stable and would not have reacted with anything. Knowing that most CFCs had been released in the Northern Hemisphere, Dr. Lovelock reasoned that their whereabouts could tell us something about the circulation of air in the atmosphere. His research led other scientists working in the early 1970s to discover that CFCs rise through the atmosphere and into the ozone layer. There they are exposed to increased ultraviolet radiation. This breaks apart the CFC molecule, releasing its carbon, fluoride, and chlorine atoms. The chlorine atoms react with ozone and destroy it in a chain reaction. This means that each chlorine atom may react with and destroy thousands of ozone molecules.

This was an alarming discovery. In 1973, it was estimated that about one and a half billion pounds of CFCs had been released into the atmosphere, and an increasing amount was being added every year. Not only were CFCs floating into the air from spray cans, foams, and manufacturing processes, they were released every time a leak occurred in the cooling system of an air conditioner or refrigerator. When these appliances were disposed of at the local dump, people had no way of knowing that the leaking CFCs in the coolant would bubble up into the stratosphere where they would linger for over a century, damaging the ozone layer.

Although CFCs were the largest problem, damage to the ozone layer was also caused by other gases. Some fire extinguishers that are used to put out fires of flammable liquids, such as gasoline, contain halons, a mixture of gases that, like

CFCs, are manufactured in an industrial process. However, halons are much more destructive to the ozone layer per pound than CFCs. Their production is now banned in the United States. Existing supplies of halons are not used during firefighter exercises as in the past but are saved for actual emergencies.

Nitrous oxide is a gas that is like CFCs in that it is both a greenhouse gas and it nibbles away at the ozone layer. But unlike CFCs, this gas is found in nature. It is produced from a variety of sources: bacteria in the soil, forest fires, erupting volcanoes, and decaying plants. In the past century the concentration of nitrous oxide in the atmosphere has increased by about 10 percent.

Many scientists believe this increase in nitrous oxide is not the result of natural forces, but rather of human activities. Agriculture is the source of some nitrous oxide. When chemical fertilizers are applied to land, nitrous oxide forms in the air. Nitrous oxide is also formed by burning wood and fossil fuels. Household furnaces, factories, electric power plants, airplanes, and motor vehicles all contribute to the nitrous oxide that circulates to the upper atmosphere. There it builds up in the stratosphere and destroys the ozone layer.

The amount of ozone loss experienced in a particular location depends on latitude and season. Most of the world's people live between 30 degrees and 64 degrees north latitude. This includes most of the United States, Canada, Europe, Russia and the Commonwealth of Independent States, China, and Japan. In 1993, the lowest recorded levels of ozone were measured to date, not just at the poles, but at populated mid-latitudes. During the winter months these losses were as high as 15 percent. They were much larger than predicted by computer modeling.

Above Anchorage, Alaska, which is 60 degrees north latitude, ozone loss has been measured at 8.3 percent over the past decade. The EPA estimates that for every 1 percent loss in ozone there is a 2 percent increase in ultraviolet radiation reaching the Earth. The increase in ultraviolet radiation from a 10 percent loss in ozone where you live would be equivalent to moving 30 degrees closer to the equator. For example, if you live in Anchorage and 10 percent of the ozone layer were destroyed there, you would get as much ultraviolet radiation as someone who lives in Orlando, Florida.

In the mid-1980s British scientists discovered a gaping hole in the ozone layer over Antarctica. Since that time every spring, the hole has grown and spread. By 1986 it had spread as far south as 50 degrees south latitude, near the tip of South America and not far from Australia. By the spring of 1991 the hole was as large as the entire North American continent and deeper than Mount McKinley (Denali), the highest mountain in North America, is high.

Antarctica's frigid climate and a system of winds that whirl around the pole for much of the winter cause the greater thinning of the ozone layer at the South Pole. Winter there occurs during our warmer months, from May to August. During that time the Antarctic is very cold and dark. The sun stays below the horizon all day long. The intense cold causes scarce water vapor in the atmosphere to freeze and form ice crystals. These frozen crystals make up a special kind of icy cloud that does not form in temperate latitudes. Chlorine compounds attach to the ice crystals. With the first light of the Antarctic spring, the crystals melt and the chlorine atoms that destroy the ozone layer are released. By late October, strong winds from the temperate zone bring ozone-rich air to Antarctica, closing the hole.

At the North Pole, the milder winter conditions account for the fact that seasonal spring ozone loss is much less than at the South Pole. Average Arctic temperatures are 20 degrees warmer than in Antarctica, so the icy clouds that form are not

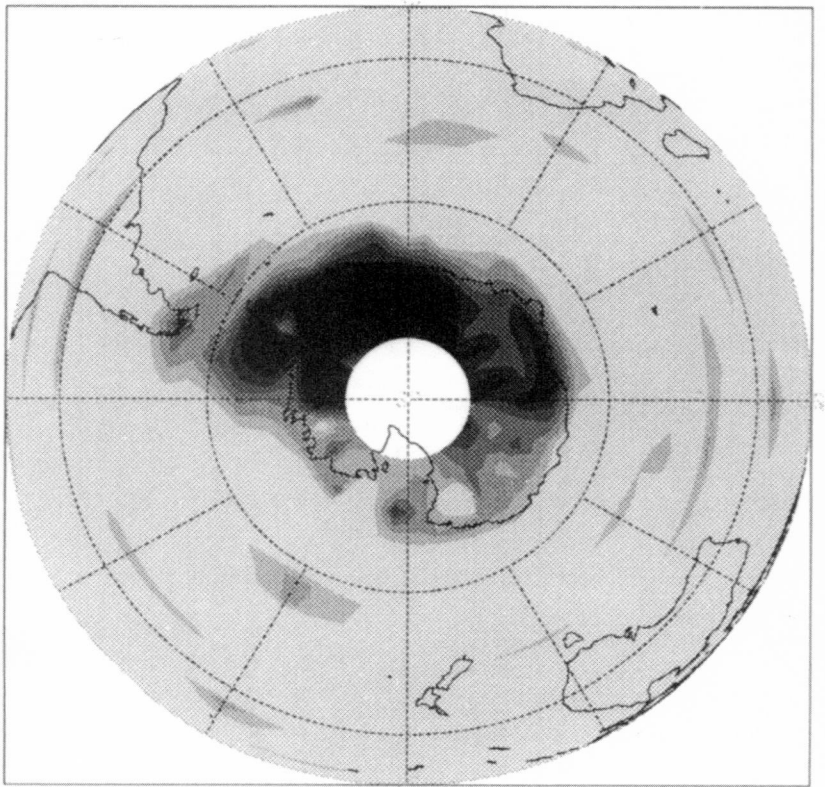

Dark areas show high concentrations of chlorine molecules over the Southern Hemisphere. Lighter areas show lower concentrations. CREDIT: NASA

as extensive nor as long lasting.

Antarctica is a natural laboratory for studying Earth's atmosphere and climate. It is the only continent where no civilization has been established and it is far removed from industrial sources of pollution. Except where the Antarctic peninsula extends toward South America, it is more then 2,000 miles from any other continent. This isolation from populated areas is reinforced by the harsh climate of the South Pole. All but 5 percent of Antarctica is covered by glaciers. Because it is so difficult to explore, far less is known

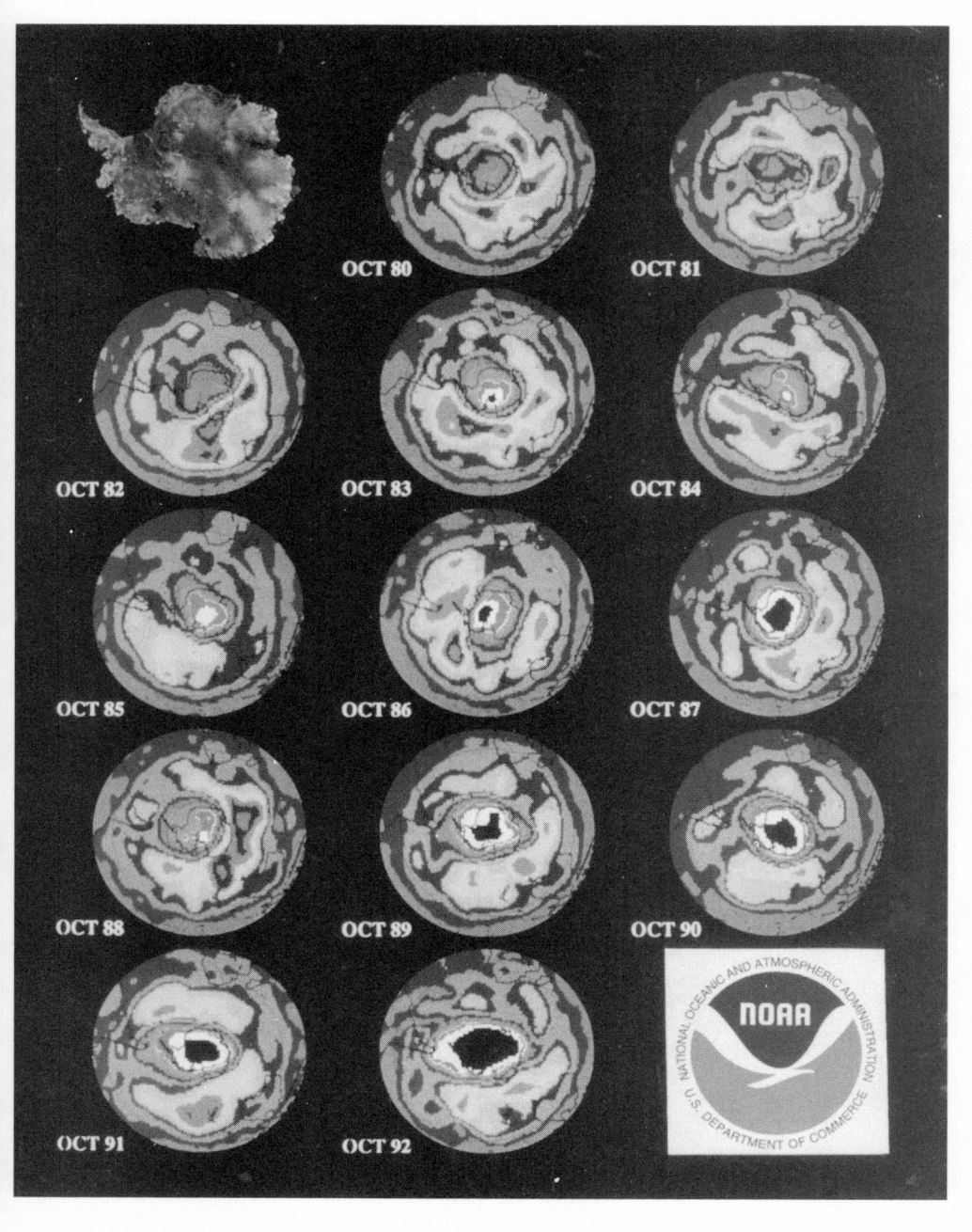

This computer drawing shows the enlarging Antarctic ozone hole as a growing black spot from the years 1980–1992. CREDIT: U.S. DEPARTMENT OF COMMERCE, NOAA

A cargo plane with skis lands on a snow-packed runway in Antarctica. CREDIT: NATIONAL SCIENCE FOUNDATION. PHOTO BY ANN HAWTHORNE

about this continent than any other. The water that surrounds Antarctica, sometimes referred to as the Antarctic Ocean, has a temperature of 29 degrees, colder than any other ocean on Earth, and is renowned for its stormy seas.

Today the United States Antarctica Research Program's main base is McMurdo Station on Ross Island in McMurdo Sound. There scientists conduct research in the harsh Antarctic climate to find out more about the ozone hole and how it affects living things.

At McMurdo Station, one of the problems scientists are studying is the effect the hole in the ozone layer may have on living things. It is known that increased ultraviolet radiation causes people's skin to sunburn more easily. This results in leathery and wrinkled skin that shows signs of early aging. It also increases the incidence of skin cancer. Ultraviolet rays may also affect people's and animals' ability to resist disease. They also cause cataracts, a clouding of the lens of the eye, which can cause blindness if left untreated. Increased ultraviolet radiation may interfere with photosynthesis, and crops may not grow as well.

Scientists are particularly concerned about the effect of increased radiation on phytoplankton in Antarctic waters. Phytoplankton need sunlight for photosynthesis. But if the ultraviolet rays are too intense, phytoplankton, especially in the upper 50 feet of the ocean, do not thrive. Phytoplankton are the basis of the marine **food chain**. These plants are eaten by small marine animals, such as krill, tiny shrimp-like

65

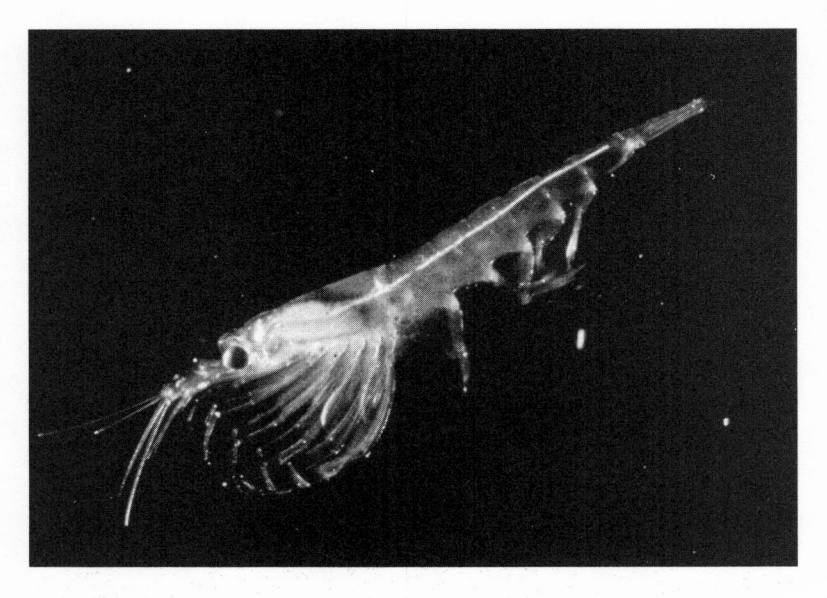

This krill is an important food source for larger marine animals. It is shown in a feeding position. Its primary food is phytoplankton. CREDIT: NATIONAL SCIENCE FOUNDATION

animals. Krill in turn are food for larger ocean dwellers, including some species of whales, penguins, birds, fish, seals, and squid. The survival of phytoplankton is crucial to the survival of the entire Antarctic marine ecosystem.

Scientists at McMurdo also monitor the atmosphere using research balloons, satellites, and specially equipped planes. Since 1957, when a giant helium-filled balloon carried instruments high above the Earth, balloons have been used to measure ozone levels in the upper atmosphere. Because they are blown by the winds, their flight paths are difficult to control and often they have been lost with all of the expensive instruments on board.

Now information about the atmosphere is also collected by satellites and specially equipped planes. The Nimbus 7 satellite, launched by NASA in 1978, obtains weather information. As it passed over Antarctica in the mid-1980s, data it later produced showed levels of ozone over the continent had dropped by half. This confirmed the earlier results of the British scientists. However, these findings were so startling that scientists questioned whether the information was accurate. Astronauts on board the space shuttle *Atlantis* studied Earth's atmosphere in 1992. Their journey was extended an extra day so that they could collect additional information about the thinning of the ozone layer.

In 1986, data gathered by a team of scientists pointed toward CFCs as the most likely cause of the ozone hole. By the late 1980s a project involving NASA, the National Science Foundation, and the National Oceanic and Atmospheric Administration confirmed the existence of the ozone hole and the role of CFCs in causing it. They used a special aircraft, the ER-2, a modified single-engine spy plane to probe the ozone layer. With its long, slender wings, the ER-2 resembles a glider and can be airborne for a maximum of eight hours. It can fly at altitudes of up to 70,000 feet

Launching a high-altitude balloon at McMurdo Station. CREDIT: NATIONAL SCIENCE FOUNDATION. PHOTO BY JULIE PALAIS

67

(about 13 miles) through the lower part of the ozone hole. The ER-2 is equipped with sensitive instruments to sample ozone and chlorine levels and analyze the icy clouds. The highly trained, courageous NASA pilot is alone in the ER-2's single seat in the cramped cockpit. Pilots trained for these important missions have flown out of Punta Arenas, Chile, to study the ozone hole in Antarctica; and out of Stavanger, Norway; Fairbanks, Alaska; and Bangor, Maine, to study the ozone over the Arctic. Flying conditions are dangerous due to the high winds in polar regions and the extreme cold at high altitudes.

Because the ER-2 can only poke at the bottom of the upper stratosphere and cannot obtain the detailed information that is needed, scientists are developing new high-flying unmanned planes called drones to study the upper atmosphere. Drones are controlled from the ground, and the first high-altitude mission will undoubtedly be accomplished by a drone called *Perseus*, which will be operated by an onboard computer. It is named after a hero in Greek mythology who rode Pegasus, a winged horse, across the sky.

Perseus is a major step forward in our ability to study the atmosphere. It is being developed by about thirty engineers and scientists at Aurora Flight Sciences, a company in northeastern Virginia. Scientists hope that *Perseus* will be able to fly 15 to 20 miles up toward the ozone hole when it is completed. They anticipate that sensors mounted on the aircraft's nose will respond when it enters the icy stratospheric Antarctic clouds. Then, computers on board will activate air sampling devices. The entire flight will last about six hours.

The Aurora Ground Station will be the mission control center during the *Perseus* flight. It contains work stations for the land-based pilot-operator and several engineers. By watching three computer screens, the pilot-operator will be able to monitor flight information such as airspeed and altitude, trace the aircraft's location along its programmed flight path, and see video images from the aircraft's nose camera. The pilot-operator can communicate with the onboard com-

Perseus A, *a high-flying drone that will be used to study the upper atmosphere.*
CREDIT: AURORA FLIGHT SCIENCES CORPORATION

puters by ultra-high-frequency radio.

Because of the serious consequences of the destruction of the ozone layer, in the late 1970s the United States banned CFCs from aerosol cans. However, even if the production and use of CFCs were completely stopped today, there would not be an immediate solution to the problem. It takes CFCs several years to percolate through the atmosphere to the ozone layer, and they have a lifespan there of from 50 to 400 years.

In 1987 more than forty nations sent delegates to a conference in Montreal, Canada. Industrialized nations agreed to phase out CFC production. In June 1990 another agreement established a 100 percent ban by 2000, with allowances for developing nations. At subsequent international meetings, industrialized nations agreed to stop CFC production as of the end of 1995. Exceptions were made for developing nations and special uses such as in medicine. Since the 1987 conference, one hundred more nations have signed this agreement, called the Montreal Protocol.

Furthermore, the Clean Air Act was amended in 1990 to include an ozone protection program. CFCs tend to leak out of automobile air-conditioning systems as they age. In past years some people, rather than getting the system properly repaired, refilled the coolant as it leaked away. Since November 1992, the Clean Air Act amendments prohibit containers of CFC coolant from being sold to anyone but a certified technician. In January 1993, the first penalties in the nation were levied, in New England, for illegal sales of CFCs in auto parts stores, hardware stores, and national chain stores. Fines ranged from seven thousand to thirty thousand dollars.

The Clean Air Act amendments require that certain pro-

cedures be followed when automobile air-conditioning units are serviced. In the past it was common for a service station attendant to drain the coolant containing CFCs and let it evaporate into the air. Now mechanics who repair air-conditioning must be trained and certified by an EPA-approved organization. They are required to use special recover/recycle machines to capture the coolant and transfer it to a holding tank. Then it is either recycled and returned to the car's air-conditioning after repairs or sent to a facility for purification so that it can be used again.

New products are being developed to phase out the use of CFCs. New, safer coolants containing hydrofluorocarbons (HFCs) are widely available and are used in all motor vehicles manufactured in the United States today. The air-conditioning systems of older cars need to be adapted before they can run on the new coolants. Manufacturers are developing experimental refrigerators that use a helium cooling system. A real challenge exists in producing insulating foams that are as economical and efficient as those made with CFCs. HFCs are just as damaging to the ozone layer as CFCs. However they are less stable so fewer HFCs survive into the upper atmosphere.

In spite of current research, there is still much to be learned about the relationship between CFCs and the ozone layer. The challenge lies in finding ways to maintain a balance between the modern conveniences that are part of our daily lives and protecting the atmosphere.

CHAPTER FIVE

RESCUING EARTH'S ATMOSPHERE— VISIONS OF AN EXCITING NEW ENERGY FUTURE

The problems with our atmosphere that you have read about—air pollution, acid rain, increasing greenhouse gases, and ozone depletion—are all the result of human activities. As you have learned, most of the energy we use today comes from fossil fuels. When they are burned to produce energy, they emit polluting gases that affect natural ecosystems. Now many people are realizing that the conveniences of the twentieth century must be reexamined in light of what their ultimate cost to the environment may be. It is not practical to think of going without heating, air-conditioning, automobiles, refrigerators, and freezers. However, it is possible to design new **technologies** that are less polluting. Technology is the use of science in solving problems.

Fossil fuels that have been formed over millions of years are **nonrenewable** resources. When coal, oil, and natural gas are burned, their energy is used up and cannot be replaced. Therefore, by depending on fossil fuels as our primary source of energy, we are both polluting the air and depleting their supply. Even now, the United States cannot supply enough oil to meet its needs. For this reason, we must import it from other countries. Our dependence on foreign oil draws us into international conflicts such as the Persian Gulf War.

One way of lessening our dependence on fossil fuels is to use noncarbon-based fuels such as nuclear energy. Nuclear energy was once viewed by its supporters as the ultimate answer to the nation's energy needs. However, it has encountered many problems since the first commercial operating plant was built in 1957 in Shippingport, Pennsylvania. Nuclear refers to the center or **nucleus** of an atom, the smallest unit of an element. If the nucleus of an atom can be split, tremendous amounts of energy are released. Scientists have found ways to split certain large nuclei, such as that of uranium. The heat produced in the nuclear power reactor is used to generate electricity in a way similar to a power plant that burns fossil fuels. However, because nothing is burned to produce the heat, gases that lead to the formation of smog and acid rain as well as those that produce a greenhouse effect are not emitted. However, while nuclear power is kinder to the atmosphere, other factors must be considered.

Uranium, the fuel used in the production of nuclear power, is **radioactive**. This means that it gives off rays that can be harmful to living things. Special precautions must be taken to protect the workers in the plant and the environment outside the plant from the radioactivity. Some waste materials from nuclear reactors remain radioactive for hundreds of thousands of years and facilities for storing them are presently inadequate. An additional danger is that these wastes can be used to manufacture nuclear weapons. The future of nuclear energy may lie in the development of new reactors that are safer and cheaper to build and operate.

Perhaps in the future, more of our energy will come from **renewable** sources. These are things that can be used over and over again, without depleting their energy. They are even better because they can be found in the United States. **Biofuels**, the energy that comes from burning once-living things, are renewable forms of energy. Native Americans and later the European colonists burned wood to warm their dwellings and cook their food. Even now, the great majority of people in developing countries cook food with biofuels using the energy of burning wood, straw, or dung. In industrialized countries, some power plants, such as the one in Burlington, Vermont, are fired by wood. Other cities, such as Tuscaloosa, Alabama, are burning garbage to produce heat to generate electricity. The smoke from too many wood-burning operations in one area can cause its own air pollution, however.

Hydropower, the energy of moving water, is a renewable energy source that Americans have used for over two hundred years. The force of falling water was used to rotate flat stones between which grain was crushed. Today hydropower is used to turn the shaft of a generator to produce electricity in hydroelectric power plants. Two such plants are located at the Hoover Dam on the Colorado River between Arizona and Nevada and at Niagara Falls on the boundary between the United States and Canada. Although hydropower does not produce harmful gases, it affects the environment in other ways. Building a dam across a river disrupts the migration of fish, changes the temperature of the water so that it is unsuitable for some fish species, and floods forest and farmland when the reservoir forms.

The sun is the Earth's primary energy source. Shining from 92 million miles away, the sun provides an unlimited supply of energy that is clean and free. More energy comes from the sun in just a few minutes than people all over the world use in a year! In the broadest sense, all our energy comes from the sun. The plants that grew during prehistoric times and were food for the dinosaurs got their energy from the sun. These, and all the animals that fed upon them, formed the fossil fuels when they died and were compressed under layers of rock and mud. The sun is also the energy that powers the water cycle. It causes water from oceans, lakes, and rivers to evaporate and return to the Earth in the form of rain and snow. This cycle keeps the water flowing in rivers.

However, when we speak of energy from the sun, or **solar** energy, we are usually referring to capturing the sun's heat or light energy directly. The idea of solar energy is not new. In fact the word *solar* comes from Sol, the name ancient Romans gave to their sun god. Since ancient times, people have known that the energy from the sun could be used to warm water. Almost one thousand years ago, the Anasazi people of northeastern Arizona used solar energy to heat living spaces, a practice that is increasingly common today. They built their dwellings on ledges in cliff faces to capture the warmth of the low winter sun. The overhanging cliffs also provided shade from the intense summer sun.

Everything exposed to the sun is a solar collector. When you are riding your bike outdoors, the hot asphalt road beneath your tires and the trees on your street are all solar collectors. Plants are called perfect solar collectors because they efficiently absorb, store, and use the sun's energy through photosynthesis.

Architects often design houses and buildings to be solar collectors. Perhaps you have seen solar houses. They are built with lots of windows on the sunny southern side. These windows have overhanging roofs designed to shade the windows from the hot summer sun when it is higher in the sky than it is in the winter. The heat of the sun streaming through the windows is captured and stored by something in the house. It might be a dark brick or slate floor, or perhaps drums of water. As the sun sets, and the house begins to cool, the trapped heat warms the house. On the darker, northern side

Solar house showing thermal solar collectors on south-facing roof. CREDIT: ACORN STRUCTURES, INC., CONCORD, MA

of the house, there are few windows and the walls are thickly insulated. A system like this is called passive solar heating because it has no moving parts that circulate the heat.

Solar heating systems that use mechanical means such as fans and pumps to move heat from one place to another are called active solar systems. In most cases, the **thermal** collectors for these systems are placed on a south-facing roof of the building. They are sighted at the proper angle, determined by the latitude of the building, for maximum exposure to the sun.

The collector panels are insulated weatherproof boxes. They contain a dark-colored absorbing plate covered by a transparent glass or plastic sheet that traps the heat. The heat absorbed by the collector is transferred by air or water that is pumped through it. Most commonly, water or antifreeze circulates in a closed pipe system through both the collector and a water tank. The liquid leaves the collector and flows through the water storage tank where its heat is absorbed by cooler water. It then returns to the collector to be reheated. Usually the water in the storage tank circulates through a building's radiators to provide heat. Often, gas or oil can be burned in a furnace to provide back-up heat in these systems.

In addition to space heating, active solar systems can be used to heat water for a building. These are similar but smaller versions of the active space heating systems. Water circulates in a loop through the solar collector and the hot water tank. The heat the water absorbs from the collectors is transferred to the water in the tank. These systems also often require additional heat to keep the water at about 140 degrees on cold or dark days.

Active solar systems can also be used to heat the water in swimming pools, usually to a temperature of about 80 degrees. In these systems, the pool water is pumped through the filter and then through the solar collectors. There it absorbs the sun's heat before returning to the pool. In many areas, using solar hot water systems can extend the number of months a pool can be used.

Climate greatly influences how practical a solar thermal energy system is. In northern latitudes the days are short in the winter and the weather is often cloudy. Southern parts of the United States where there is intense sunlight for more of the year are able to produce more solar energy.

Scientists and engineers are developing ways to use the heat of the sun to produce electricity. An example of this is the Solar One Pilot Plant near Barstow, California. It is comprised of 1,800 special mirrors called heliostats. They reflect sunlight onto a receiver atop a 300-foot "power tower." Each mirror must be programmed so that it tracks the movement of the sun across the sky. The focused sunlight produces intense heat (about 1,050 degrees) that boils a liquid and produces steam. The steam is used to turn a shaft and produce electricity, just as it is in a conventional power plant. Solar thermal production is a clean, reliable source of electricity that produces no emissions. Scientists, governments, and private industry are working together to develop new technologies such as the power tower.

You may be familiar with another way in which the energy of the sun can be used to produce electricity. It involves the use of **photovoltaic** or solar cells that convert sunlight directly into electrical energy. Perhaps you have seen photovoltaic cells on a calculator. The main component in a photovoltaic cell is usually three thin layers of silicon, a material found in ordinary sand. Before it can be used, the silicon must be refined to remove impurities, an expensive process. The high-quality silicon that remains produces an electric current when it absorbs light. This is direct current, the same kind as produced by batteries. A device called an inverter is needed to convert the electricity to alternating current, the kind used in electrical appliances and lighting.

An example of a demonstration project to test photovoltaic electric generating systems exists in Gardner, Massachusetts, a city about fifty miles west of Boston. There, the Massachusetts Electric Company has outfitted thirty houses and five other buildings—the city hall, library, a store, a restaurant, and the local community college—with photovoltaic systems. The solar cells are grouped together in glass weatherproof panels. These panels are installed either directly on the roofs of the buildings or on steel brackets mounted on the roofs. At first glance you might mistake the photovoltaic array for solar thermal collectors.

All the buildings in the research project are still connected by electrical wires to the Massachusetts Electric

Company. If more electricity is needed than the photo-voltaic cells can supply at a given time, additional amounts of power are automatically drawn from the utility company power grid.

While the cost of producing electricity from the sun is steadily going down, in 1993 it was still five to ten times more than from conventional sources. But more and more electric utilities are experimenting with the use of a mix of energy sources. The Solar 2000 program involves representatives of the Department of Energy (DOE), electric utilities, and industries. These people are working together to promote the use of photovoltaics. In some states the cost of new energy projects will include the cost of cleaning up environmental pollution. This will increase the cost of energy produced from fossil fuels as compared to that produced by renewable sources.

Federal and state governments can encourage and discourage use of particular energy sources. One way of doing this is with taxes, money charges on people or things that are then used for public purposes. For example, utilities might have to pay a carbon tax based on the carbon dioxide emissions they produce. In this example, electric power plants burning coal would pay the highest taxes, while those that used nonpolluting sources would pay none. Conversely, sometimes the government gives money outright or in the form of tax credits to encourage the development or improvement of energy technologies.

The National Audubon Society is an example of an environmental organization that is trying to influence the government to reform the way utilities produce electricity. They have organized the Audubon Solar Brigade, which encourages people to write to their local utility and to their elected representatives in Congress to demand that in ten years, 10 percent of electricity will be solar generated. (The campaign was begun in 1992 and the target date is therefore

2002.) Additionally, lawmakers are encouraged to guarantee that electric bills do not increase by more than 1 percent. Participating individuals are asked to send their names and addresses and the name of their local utility company to the Solar Brigade headquarters in New York. By documenting that thousands of people support 10 percent solar in ten years, public pressure is brought to bear on legislators and utilities to make the conversion to solar power feasible.

Electricity usage is measured in watt hours and is recorded by electric meters. You can probably locate the electric meter in your house or apartment. It may be outside, next to your house or garage. If it is inside, it is located where the electric utility line enters your dwelling. The flat wheel in the meter rotates whenever electrical power is drawn from the system.

An electric meter records the amount of electricity used by customers of electric utility companies. The meter is sealed inside a protective case. CREDIT: CHRISTINA G. MILLER

You can keep track of how much electricity your household is using. Record the readings on the meter's dials for a week. Read the dials at the beginning of the week and again at the end. Read the numbers from right to left and copy them in the same order. When the indicator is between two numbers, record the lower number. By subtracting the first reading from the second one, you can determine the number of watt hours used. Electric companies usually divide the watt hours by 1000 to determine the number of kilowatt hours that has been used. You can call your electric company to see how much one kilowatt hour costs to determine your electricity bill for a particular period.

Sometimes the photovoltaic cells used in the demonstration project in Gardner produce more electricity than each building can use. Then the excess power from the building flows in the opposite direction, from the customer to the utility. When this occurs the electric meter actually turns in reverse, lowering the customer's electric bill.

The power of the wind also can be harnessed to generate electricity. Wind is a kind of solar energy because the movement of air is caused by the sun heating it. As air is warmed it rises, and cool air moves in to take its place. The invisible power of the wind is all around you. You may not notice its energy when you see a flag fluttering in a gentle breeze. However, the force of wind becomes apparent when we see the destruction caused by hurricanes and tornadoes.

The energy of the wind was used hundreds of years ago to propel ships. In the nineteenth century it was used in rural areas in the American Midwest. A windmill, mounted on a tower, had a wheel with many blades like a pinwheel and a tail to turn it windward. The wind turning the wheel created mechanical energy to grind grain, saw wood, and pump water for farm families and animals. The energy in wind was also captured by windmills and used to turn an electric generator.

Wind turbines at Solaro, California, generate electricity without polluting the air. CREDIT: U.S. WINDPOWER,INC.

Today people are rediscovering the clean, reliable, free energy in the wind. However, modern wind machines or wind turbines, as they are called, bear little resemblance to the windmills that dotted the prairie two hundred years ago. Models built in the 1980s weighed several tons and some had blades as long as a football field. Others used blades similar to those designed for helicopters. The size of these huge wind turbines and others that looked like giant egg beaters made them unreliable and uncontrollable. They frequently required expensive repairs.

Wind turbines in use today are usually mounted on a tower. Their blades, resembling airplane propellers, are shorter and made out of lightweight materials such as fiberglass. Speed is controlled by a computer that activates brakes to keep it constant even in strong gusts. These modern turbines capture far more of the wind's energy than older models.

In the United States, California is leading the way in rediscovering the energy in the wind. More than 15,000 wind turbines have been erected in that state's mountain passes. There the wind funnels between the mountains, regularly blowing at speeds between 15 and 20 miles per hour. Wind turbines are clustered together in "wind farms." These are connected to a utility power grid. At good sites, energy from the wind costs about the same as power from fossil fuel plants. In 1992, reliance on wind power in California reduced power plant emissions by more than 2.5 billion pounds of carbon dioxide and millions of pounds of particulates and acid-rain-causing pollutants.

In the future as we become more knowledgeable about how to harness the power in the wind, more electricity at a cheaper cost may be produced from this important energy source. It is expected that European countries, especially Denmark, Germany, England, and the Netherlands, will rapidly expand their use of wind power. In the United States, the DOE has identified thirty-seven states with sufficient wind to support development of utilities using this source. However, wind turbines cannot replace conventional plants completely, because the wind does not always blow. But wind, unlike solar energy, is available throughout the night. Experts predict that within thirty years, wind power could supply 10 to 20 percent of the United States' energy needs. The Solar Brigade includes wind power in their message of 10 percent solar electricity in ten years.

Some homeowners have private wind turbines in their yards that produce some of the electricity they use in their homes. You may want to explore whether wind-generated electricity is practical where you live. To capture the energy in the wind, there must be a suitable open site. Like a kite, wind turbines need open land free of obstructions. They also require an average minimum wind speed of 12 miles per hour to work efficiently. You can learn about wind conditions in your area by reading the National Weather Service report in the local newspaper or by writing to the Environmental Data Service.

Many of the problems in the atmosphere come from our dependence on gasoline-powered motor vehicles to move passengers and goods from one place to another. Gasoline-powered engines were first developed in the late 1800s. However, it was not until 1914 that Henry Ford built the Model T on an assembly line. This mass production brought the car's cost within reach of many people, not just the wealthy.

Now, less than one hundred years later, cars are the basis for the mobile society in which we live. While the United States has only 5 percent of the world's population, its citizens account for half the miles driven worldwide! Americans have doubled their driving mileage in the last fifteen years, and many families have more than one car. This increase has offset the reduction in pollution emissions that otherwise would have occurred due to cleaner burning and more efficient engines. However, the air pollution motor vehicles produce is providing the impetus for developing new kinds of cars that produce zero or greatly reduced emissions.

People from middle school students to senior engineers in the world's largest automobile companies are developing these new technologies. If you are a seventh- or eighth-grade student you may want to participate in the Junior Solar Sprint. This is an annual competition sponsored by the DOE in which students use their knowledge of math and science as well as their creativity to design small model solar cars. Participating schools are sent Junior Solar Sprint car kits free of charge. The kits contain solar cells and a motor. Students must supply their own design for the body, wheels, and guidewires that steer the cars. The Junior Solar Sprint

Students monitor their vehicles, powered by energy from photovoltaic cells, in the Junior Solar Sprint. CREDIT: U.S. DEPARTMENT OF ENERGY

competition is held in the spring in regions throughout the country. Prizes are awarded for both best design and speed.

College students may enter the DOE-sponsored Sunrayce, a long-distance race held every two years in which participants race full-size solar cars they have built. To be eligible to enter Sunrayce, teams composed of science, math, and engineering students submit a proposal. It outlines their plan to design and build a single-seat solar car that uses the sun as its only source of power. An array of photovoltaic cells on the car produces the electrical energy that powers it. This electricity either goes directly to the motor when the car is running or recharges the batteries when the car is idle.

In 1993 teams from thirty-six colleges were selected to participate in Sunrayce. Each received several thousand dollars from the EPA and DOE for materials needed to build their solar cars. A recent race began in Dallas, Texas, and followed a course through Fort Worth, Oklahoma City, Tulsa, Kansas City, and finished in Minneapolis-St. Paul, a distance of approximately 1,000 miles.

In addition to Sunrayce, there are worldwide solar car competitions such as the Tour de Sol held in France, Switzerland, and the United States, and the Solar Challenge in Australia. Some of the entries to these races are modified conventional cars with photovoltaic cells mounted on the roof. Other cars look like something you might see only in a cartoon or comic strip. Some look like oversized cookie sheets that are covered with solar cells and supported by wheels. These cars have a plastic bubble for the driver to sit in.

Ordinarily you wouldn't expect to see a racing car pulled over to the side of the road during a race unless it was having mechanical problems. However, some solar cars need to do

A finalist in a recent American Tour de Sol. CREDIT: NORTHEAST SUSTAINABLE ENERGY ASSOCIATION. PHOTO BY C. MICHAEL LEWIS

this to soak up sunlight and recharge their batteries. By building these cars and driving them under actual road conditions, students learn a great deal about using energy from the sun for transportation. These "high tech" solar racing cars are the forerunners of new breeds of automobiles that do not produce gases that harm the atmosphere.

A different kind of electric car is being developed by major automobile companies all over the world. Rather than getting their power from the sun, these cars contain batteries that are recharged by being plugged into an electric socket. Their energy, therefore, is produced by conventional sources. They are called EVs (electric vehicles). If you have seen a golf cart or an electric wheelchair, then you have seen an EV. They are any form of transportation that is operated by an electric motor in which the electricity is stored in a battery.

As the electric motor of an EV runs, it produces no emissions. Because there are no tailpipe emissions, carbon dioxide and other greenhouse gases are not produced. When these are in use, city air will be much cleaner and people who live in Los Angeles, for example, will again have a clear view of the countryside. However, the amount of pollutants emitted from power plants that produce electricity used by EVs will not improve. Therefore, EVs cannot be regarded as a form of transportation that has no negative effect on the atmosphere. Nevertheless, emissions from stationary sources like power plants can be more easily controlled than those from millions of vehicles. If an EV were recharged using electricity produced by renewable sources, it would not harm the atmosphere.

California, the state with the most severe air pollution, is in the process of adopting the toughest emission laws in the nation. California law requires that by 1998, 2 percent of each manufacturer's new cars be emission-free. This number will increase to 10 percent by the year 2003. Laws such as these and pressure from citizen groups are leading to intense

General Motor's EV, the Impact 3, seats two people and has power windows, door locks, side mirrors, dual airbags, cruise control, AM/FM stereo radio/cassette/ CD player, and power steering. It can travel about 100 miles before its batteries need recharging. CREDIT: GENERAL MOTORS ELECTRIC VEHICLE PROGRAM

worldwide competition among automobile manufacturers to produce affordable, zero-emission cars.

The three major U.S. automakers—Ford, Chrysler, and General Motors—are pouring research dollars into EV development and are building prototype electric cars. On January 1, 1993, General Motors' sporty two-seater EV, the Impact 3, led the 104th Tournament of Roses parade in Pasadena, California. Imagine that you are invited to be a passenger in the car and come along for a ride. The first thing you might notice is how quiet the car is. As you travel the parade route, you can hear the applause of the crowds. Then, glancing at the instrument panel on the dashboard, you would not see a fuel gauge. In its place is a voltmeter, a dial that indicates how much electricity is stored in the batteries. Since there is an electric motor instead of a gasoline engine under the hood, there is no engine temperature gauge. There is no exhaust pipe because no emissions are produced. And because the Impact does not use oil, there is no oil gauge. For refueling, you would connect the socket-end of a heavy duty extension cord to a built-in plug behind the fuel-filler door. Connecting the cord to an electrical outlet that provides 220 volts of household current recharges the Impact's batteries. This is the same kind of current that is used in electric clothes dryers and stoves.

In June of 1995, the *Vineyard Gazette*, a newspaper published on the island of Martha's Vineyard, Massachusetts, printed an article about Martha, the island's new electric

Martha, the electric shuttle bus, is used to transport people between a ferry terminal and a parking lot a mile and a half away. CREDIT: M. C. WALLO.

shuttle bus. Martha was built in California to demonstrate the reliability of electric buses. She is now used to provide transportation between a Martha's Vineyard ferry terminal and a parking lot about a mile and a half away. Most of the island's visitors and residents never have ridden in an electric bus before, because there are so few of them in operation.

Martha is 97 percent cleaner to operate than a conventional bus. A digital screen shows Martha's drivers how much electrical energy is stored in the battery and how much is used on each run. After Martha completes her ten-hour workday, her batteries are recharged for about six hours.

Compared to conventional buses, electric buses have fewer moving parts, require less time for maintenance, and last longer. However, currently, electric buses can travel only about 75 miles before needing recharging, and they are more expensive to buy. Transportation planners expect that future improvements in electric buses will bring their costs down and increase their popularity. Nationwide, Santa Barbara, California, has the largest daily fleet of electric buses. It is the oldest continuous operator of these vehicles in the United States, with a system begun in 1991.

EVs are really a "new old" idea. Electric cars were the most popular cars in America at the turn of the century. They were safer, cleaner, and quieter than the steam-powered cars that preceded them. However, they were slow in gathering speed. Most could not travel faster than about 20 miles per hour, and their batteries had to be recharged about every 50 miles. For these reasons, electric cars were abandoned in favor of the more versatile, powerful, and reliable automobiles that ran on gasoline.

Although the batteries in today's EVs have made enormous improvements over those of the early 1900s, their safety and efficiency are still of concern. The key to building an EV for mass production lies in developing an advanced battery. Ford, General Motors, and Chrysler are working together to develop a new and improved EV battery. The U.S. government is supporting this effort by providing hundreds of millions of dollars annually. All around the world, companies are working to produce new, efficient, and safe EV batteries.

Modern EVs can reach speeds of 75 miles per hour. The best EVs can travel only about 120 miles before they need several hours of recharging. Although most commuter trips are far less than this, people often use their cars for longer vacations and weekend trips. At this point in their development, EVs may be best suited for use as commuter cars or for fleet vehicles, such as those used by the Post Office or other delivery services. In each of these cases, the vehicles are used only during the day and travel short distances. This would leave plenty of time for recharging during the night—a time when demand for electricity is low and some utilities charge less for it.

Imagine that all the cars in your area were EVs. Even if you lived near a highway, you would hear little traffic noise. Garage mechanics would no longer change oil and perform emissions tests. Instead, they would be trained to fix electric motors. You would have a special 220 voltage outlet in your garage or where your car was parked at night. Perhaps your garage or carport roof would support an array of photovoltaic cells. If you were away from home and your car's battery needed recharging you might drive into a "recharging station." It would have a series of metered electrical outlets. Public garages, shopping malls, city streets, and parking lots would also provide metered electric outlets. After you had inserted your credit card, you would be able to plug your car into one of them. Perhaps while you were having dinner at a restaurant or watching a movie at the theater, the plugged-in EV would be having its battery recharged!

Like EVs, alternative-fuel vehicles, meaning those that run

on nongasoline fuels, are being developed worldwide. Next to EVs, the cars that produce the fewest emissions run on natural gas. This fuel costs only about two-thirds as much as gasoline and is very plentiful.

Some cars, called flexible-fuel cars, will be able to run either on gasoline or biofuels called methanol and ethanol. Methanol is an alcohol made from wood, coal, and agricultural wastes. Ethanol is an alcohol made from grains such as corn. Building refueling stations where drivers of these vehicles can obtain alternative fuels is as essential as recharging stations are to EVs. Already in California it is possible to drive from Sacramento to San Diego and keep the tank refilled with methanol. While methanol and ethanol have the advantage of being renewable resources, each is highly corrosive and flammable. Cars that use these fuels can also be difficult to start in cold weather. Methanol produces fewer smog-producing emissions than gasoline but more carbon dioxide. While ethanol has the advantage of producing fewer greenhouse gases than gasoline, it emits a chemical that speeds up ground-level ozone formation.

Expanding public transportation systems to include many different kinds of vehicles can also help to reduce air pollution. Organized car pools and van pools, buses, underground subways (rapid rail), streetcars, and trolleys (light rail) all produce less air pollution per passenger than the single car with one occupant. Some companies encourage van pooling by paying for part or all of its costs for their employees. Some offer "guaranteed ride home programs." These allow users to take taxis or rental cars home in case of emergencies. Their companies will reimburse them for a specified number of trips each year.

Rapid and light rail systems run on electric motors, so like EVs there are no tailpipe emissions. The Clinton administration is proposing to spend about one billion dollars to help

Bike paths promote the use of bicycles as a nonpolluting means of transportation. CREDIT: CHRISTINA G. MILLER

states build high-speed passenger rail service on heavily traveled routes. These include Washington, D.C., to Charlotte, Chicago to Milwaukee, and San Diego to San Francisco. Commuter trains such as the Los Angeles Metro Link are also being built. When it is completed, the system will be able to replace 40,000 commuter trips in private cars per peak traffic period. Its use will greatly cut automobile emissions.

Parking lots and garages make it convenient for Americans to leave their cars when they are using mass transit systems. However, in some other countries around the world signs do not say "park and ride" but rather "bike and ride." In many European countries huge populations are concentrated in cities and there are few suburbs. There, average commuting distances are half of those in the United States. This accounts for greater use of biking and public transportation.

Denmark, Japan, the Netherlands, and West Germany are

some of the places where networks of roads have been built to encourage maximum use of bicycles. When you arrive at the transit system, you can leave your bike in a secure place. Or, if you wish you can take it aboard the bus, subway, or train. Because it is not practical to use a bicycle for very long distances, it is an ideal link to a public transportation system. If commuters bike to buses, railways, and subways, millions of automobile trips are saved every day. This plays a major part in cleaning up the nation's air.

There are other areas where bicycles provide the primary means of transportation. In some developing countries, bicycles are the only alternative to walking that many people can afford. In China, there are approximately 300 million bicycles and very few people own cars. People equip their bicycles and other pedal vehicles with sidecars, trailers, and baskets. They carry everything from produce to babies through the busy cities. There are some streets with five to six lanes designated as bicycle lanes.

Because of their size and speed, cars dominate the city streets of developed countries. If cycling is to become a practical means of transportation, ways must be found for cyclists to move safely and at reasonable speeds in cities. This could be accomplished by providing separate lanes or roadways. In some European cities, cyclists are allowed to pull to the front of cars stopped for traffic lights. In others, nonessential motor vehicles are prohibited in central areas. This encourages the use of bicycles.

Using a bicycle rather than a car is one way in which each person can make a difference to our atmosphere. The bicycle has been called "the most efficient machine ever invented" and it produces no pollution! Perhaps you live in an area where you can ride your bike to school. Or maybe you can ride to team practices, music lessons, or friends' houses instead of asking for a ride. Many communities are converting old railway tracks to bike paths. These enable commuters to bike into cities and provide safe areas for recreational biking. If you believe that promoting bicycling is an important way to protect the atmosphere you may want to contact a bicycle advocacy group such as the League of American Wheelmen to see how you can get involved.

Improving energy efficiency is another major key to cleaning our atmosphere. Energy efficiency is a way of measuring the amount of energy needed to do something. About one-fifth of all electricity generated in the United States is used for lighting. The EPA's Green Lights program encourages people to switch to energy-efficient lighting. This would use less energy and reduce power plant emissions. Ninety percent of energy consumed by an incandescent bulb is given off as heat rather than light. An energy-efficient lightbulb produces more light while using fewer watts of electricity. For example, rather than using a 60-watt incandescent bulb, you could use a 15-watt compact fluorescent bulb. This would provide the same amount of light while using one-fourth as much electricity. You would also prevent the release of hundreds of pounds of pollutants over the lifetime of the bulb. If your electricity comes from a coal-burning plant, you would save over 1,400 pounds of carbon dioxide. If it comes from an oil-burning plant, you would save over 800 pounds of carbon dioxide.

In 1975, the Energy Policy and Conservation Act went into effect. It enables the DOE to require that thirteen categories of major new appliances be tested to measure their energy efficiency and be labeled accordingly. By 1990 these appliances had to meet minimum standards of energy efficiency. When you are in a store that sells refrigerators, dishwashers, clothes washers and dryers, or stoves, for example, look for the yellow and black EnergyGuide label. It will tell you the approximate cost of running a particular

Dishwasher
Capacity: Standard

ENERGYGUIDE

Estimates on the scale are based on a national average electric rate of 7.63¢ per kilowatt hour and a natural gas rate of 62.70¢ per therm.

Only standard size dishwashers are used in the scale.

Electric Water Heater

Model with lowest energy cost $54	$58 THIS MODEL	Model with highest energy cost $90

Estimated yearly energy cost

Gas Water Heater

Model with lowest energy cost $27	$33 THIS MODEL	Model with highest energy cost $52

Estimated yearly energy cost

Your cost will vary depending on your local energy rate and how you use the product. This energy cost is based on U.S. Government standard tests.

How much will this model cost you to run yearly?

with an electric water heater

Loads of dishes per week	2	4	6	8	12
Estimated yearly $ cost shown below					
Cost per kilowatt hour 2¢	$5	$10	$16	$21	$31
4¢	$10	$21	$31	$42	$62
6¢	$16	$31	$47	$62	$93
8¢	$21	$42	$62	$83	$125
10¢	$26	$52	$78	$104	$156
12¢	$31	$62	$93	$125	$187

with a gas water heater

Loads of dishes per week	2	4	6	8	12
Estimated yearly $ cost shown below					
Cost per therm (100 cubic feet) 30¢	$8	$17	$25	$33	$50
40¢	$9	$18	$27	$37	$55
50¢	$10	$20	$30	$40	$60
60¢	$11	$22	$32	$43	$65
70¢	$12	$23	$35	$47	$70
80¢	$13	$25	$37	$50	$75

Ask your salesperson or local utility for the energy rate (cost per kilowatt hour or therm) in your area, and for estimated costs if you have a propane or oil water heater.

Important Removal of this label before consumer purchase is a violation of federal law (42 U.S.C. 6302).

ED-166

This EnergyGuide shows the approximate annual cost of running a particular dishwasher as compared to other models. Notice that costs are given for water heated by both electricity and gas.

appliance as compared to other models. Most energy efficient models cost more. However, because they use less electricity, they are less expensive to operate. Refrigerators use more electricity than practically any other household appliance. This is because they run continually. Under the DOE's "Super-Efficient Refrigerator Program," manufacturers are working to build more efficient models that will use only half as much electricity.

Recycling is another way individual consumers can help to protect the atmosphere. You may already be a recycler. If you have ever passed on outgrown clothes to a younger person, you are recycling them. Or you may have made Halloween costumes from old clothes. Perhaps you save the containers that margarine comes in and reuse them to hold paper clips, thumb tacks, or safety pins.

In many communities recycling of cans, paper, and glass is required. Many businesses, schools, and families keep bins for sorting items that can be recycled. Many cafeterias have special containers for recyclable beverage containers. More than 60 billion glass containers are made every year in the United States. The primary ingredients of glass are sand, soda, and lime. They are heated in huge furnaces and shaped into containers. Some of these containers end up on your kitchen shelves filled with things like soft drinks, mayonnaise, mustard, and spaghetti sauce. If, after using a container's ingredients, you recycle the glass, you will be saving energy and keeping the atmosphere cleaner. About 25 percent less fuel is needed to produce glass from recycled crushed glass than from its raw ingredients, so far less pollution is created.

Almost any action we take that **conserves** coal, oil, or natural gas is helping to protect the atmosphere. When you dress warmly in the winter, the thermostat at your house or school can be set lower. If you carry your lunch to school in a reusable cloth bag, the plastic bag the bread came in, or a

AIR ALERT

Many communities have curbside recycling programs. This truck picks up sorted cans, paper, and glass. CREDIT: LOUISE A. BERRY

98

lunch box, you're saving energy that would be used to make disposable bags. When you turn off a light in an unoccupied room, less electricity is used. By shopping for products that have minimal packaging and using bags and boxes only when necessary, you will be contributing to cleaner air.

We can also help to rescue the atmosphere by saving and planting trees. Many cities are planned with parks and greenways. These are areas of green plants amid the brick, concrete, and high-rise buildings. They provide cooling shade; walking, biking, and jogging trails for people; and habitat for wildlife. Greenways can lower summer temperatures of entire cities. This reduces the amount of air-conditioning needed in hot weather. The trees and plants absorb carbon dioxide and give off oxygen, reducing pollution and refreshing the air. Their leaves hold particulate pollutants such as dust and smoke. The pores in the leaf surfaces absorb gaseous pollutants.

RESCUING EARTH'S ATMOSPHERE

Perhaps you would like to start a tree-planting program in your neighborhood or at your school. Find out from your county extension service, nature center, nursery, or park department what species of trees grow best and are native to where you live. In 1991, President George Bush proposed a program calling for the planting of one billion trees a year nationwide. By writing to the U.S. Department of Agriculture you can find out how you can participate in the National Tree Program.

Many experts are concerned that the destruction of tropical rain forests is endangering our atmosphere. Every day thousands of acres of trees are cut down or burned. The burning contributes carbon dioxide to the atmosphere. And the destruction of the trees means that they are no longer able to cleanse the air. You can get involved with saving tropical rain forests by becoming a member of the Rainforest Action Network. For a small fee this organization will send you their publications just for students. They will even help you find a pen pal who lives in the tropical areas of Central or South America.

Some Arctic areas too are threatened. Because of our dependence on fossil fuels, pressure is building to explore for oil and gas in unspoiled areas that provide habitat for wildlife. The Arctic National Wildlife refuge in northeastern Alaska is one such area. It is a fragile, frozen area of forests, tundra, and icy seas that is rich in biodiversity. It is a sanctuary for polar bears, arctic foxes, wolves, caribou, Dall sheep, grizzly bears, and many species of birds that are well adapted to this cold environment. If industrial activities occur in this area, the survival of these animals may be at risk.

The polar bear, a majestic symbol of the Arctic, is one animal that may be threatened. Perhaps you have seen polar bears at the zoo. Mature males can weigh more than 1,500 pounds and are between 6 and 7.5 feet tall. Polar bears are well adapted to the Arctic. Their thick white or yellowish fur insulates them from the bitter cold. The front claws of these marine mammals are slightly webbed, so they are excellent swimmers. Polar bears lead solitary lives. Sometimes they ride drifting pieces of ice in the Arctic Ocean to travel from one place to another.

Drilling for oil and gas, which involves the use of explosives, helicopters, planes, bulldozers, trucks, and building of roads and pipelines, interferes with the bears' ability to reproduce and raise their young. Global warming could further threaten their survival. Exploring for and producing oil and natural gas emits thousands of tons of greenhouse gases such as methane and nitrous oxide. If polar ice decreases, this melting could cause a change in the direction of ocean

A polar bear and her cub drifting on Arctic ice. CREDIT: ANNA E. ZUCKERMAN/ TOM STACK & ASSOCIATES

currents. This would alter the kinds of plants and animals that live in the Arctic region. Seal populations could be disrupted because some of their favorite foods, fish and squid, might be scarce. If seals were not readily available, the polar bear would have to do without a source of food that normally makes up about 90 percent of its diet.

As we face the twenty-first century, it is important that we consider how our way of life will affect the atmosphere. The worldwide population is now more than five billion, and it is expected to grow to eight and a half billion by 2025. Experts predict that today's 500 million registered automobiles will quadruple in that same period. The explosion of population coupled with development in poorer nations will mean that more people are using more energy. We must make our choices wisely to protect the envelope of air that surrounds us. In rescuing the atmosphere, we will be protecting not only our own well-being but that of all other species as well.

Following are excerpts from a speech made by Congressman Gerry E. Studds in Rochester, Massachusetts, during a celebration of Earth Day 1992.

"What's biodiversity? Well, it's a fancy way of saying that it takes all kinds to make a world. Of saying that we ought not to drive animals to extinction in order to build a new shopping mall. Of saying that songbirds and shellfish and little furry things and even little crawly things have their value and their place even if you can't eat them or sell them or make sneakers out of them. Biodiversity is just a fancy way of saying that we should respect all of God's work in this world. I kind of like that and I suspect you do, too.

"You can't tell me that we lack the ability to produce energy without pollution, that we lack the technology to build more efficient cars and appliances, or that we lack the wisdom to plan better and build better and conserve more. It's not a question of whether we can; it's a question of whether we will. It's a question of whether we will meet the challenge that has confronted every generation of Americans since the Pilgrims; whether we will bequeath to our children and grandchildren a world as healthy, as beautiful, as full of life as that which we inherited upon our birth, whether that occurred ten or twenty or fifty or more years ago."

By reading this and other books about the environment you will be increasingly aware of the challenges involved in rescuing the Earth's atmosphere. Educated and informed people will be needed to implement new technologies as we enter an exciting new energy future. The coming decades could change people's lives as much as the Industrial Revolution did two hundred years ago. If each of us strives to be a caretaker rather than a consumer of the Earth, we can rescue the atmosphere. We must all do our part.

GLOSSARY

Acid—A substance with a pH of less than 7.0.

Aerosols—Particles suspended in a gas.

Algae—Simple plants that live in water and do not have roots, leaves, or flowers.

Alkalies—Bases that are dissolved in water.

Ambient—Surrounding; on all sides.

Ammonia—A colorless, sharp-smelling gas made of one part of nitrogen and three parts of hydrogen.

Atmosphere—A mass of gases surrounding a heavenly body.

Atmospheric pressure—The weight of the air that surrounds the Earth as it is pulled by gravity.

Atom—The smallest particle of an element that contains all its characteristics.

Bacteria—Single-cell organisms that are so small they can be seen only through a microscope.

Barometer—An instrument that measures atmospheric pressure.

Base—A substance with a pH of more than 7.0.

Biodiversity—The variety of living things.

Biofuels—Any kind of once-living material that is used to produce energy.

Biological—Relating to living things.

Biosphere—The part of the Earth extending from the deep crust to the atmosphere that is capable of supporting life.

Buffers—Soil, water, or bedrock that is capable of neutralizing acids and bases and offsetting changes in pH.

Climate—The average weather conditions of a place or region over a long time.

Conserves—Saves or keeps safe.

Coral—A hard, stony substance made up of the skeletons of tiny sea animals that live in tropical waters.

Corrodes—Wears away, usually over time.

Currents—Parts of the air or of a body of water that move in a certain direction.

Ecosystem—A system of relationships that exists between living and nonliving things in a particular environment.

Element—Any of the more than 100 substances that consists of atoms of only one kind and that cannot be separated into different substances by ordinary chemical means.

Environment—The air, land, water, and all the living and non-living things that make up a certain place.

Eroding—Wearing away of a land surface by wind, water, or glaciers.

Evaporates—Changes from a liquid to a gas.

Exhaust—The steam or gases that escape from an engine.

Extinction—The dying out of all members of a kind of plant or animal.

Food chain—A progression of organisms in a community in which each feeds upon the next, usually lower, member.

Fossil fuels—Fuels such as coal, oil, and natural gas that are derived from ancient plant and animal life.

Fossils—A trace or print of the remains of a plant or animal from a past age preserved in earth or rock.

Gases—Forms of matter that are neither liquid nor solid and have no shape.

Geologists—Scientists who study the natural history of the Earth through examination of its rocks and minerals.

Glaciers—Large masses of ice and snow that do not melt. Glaciers move slowly across land or down a valley until they melt or break away.

Habitat—The place where a plant or animal naturally lives and grows.

Humidity—Amount of water vapor in the air.

Hydrocarbons—Toxic substances that contain only hydrogen and carbon in various combinations.

Hydropower—Energy produced from moving water.

Hypothesis—A theory that is not proved but is assumed to be true for the purpose of further study.

Ice ages—Periods in the Earth's past when ice covered large regions of land.

Icebergs—Huge masses of ice that have broken off a glacier and are floating in the sea.

Ice caps—Thick layers of ice and snow that cover large areas of land in the polar regions or on other planets.

Ice sheets—Thick layers of ice covering a large area for a long time.

Invertebrates—Animals that do not have backbones, such as worms and insects.

Latitude—Distance measured in degrees north and south of the Earth's equator.

Marine—Pertaining to the sea.

Molecule—The smallest particle into which a substance can be divided and still maintain the characteristics of that substance. A molecule is made up of two or more atoms.

Nonrenewable—In terms of energy, something whose supply is depleted with use and cannot be replaced.

Nucleus—The center of an atom.

Photosynthesis—The process by which green plants make their own food by using the energy of sunlight, taking in water and carbon dioxide and giving off oxygen.

Photovoltaic—The direct conversion of sunlight into electricity by means of solar cells.

Phytoplankton—Tiny algae found floating in the ocean.

Pollutants—Harmful chemicals or waste materials that can damage living things.

Radioactive—Giving off energy in the form of rays that are produced by some element such as uranium.

Renewable—Capable of being replaced; a natural resource that can be replenished.

Smog—A thick haze of polluted air produced by the action of sunlight on fossil fuel emissions.

Solar—Having to do with or coming from the sun.

Technologies—The use of science in solving problems.

Thermal—Having to do with heat.

Tundra—Vast, treeless plains that exist in Arctic regions.

Ultraviolet radiation—An invisible form of short-wave radiation that can affect living things.

Universe—Everything that exists, including the Earth, the heavens, and all of space.

Vacuum—A space from which most of the air has been removed.

Visibility—The degree of clearness of the air as influenced by light, distance, and the atmosphere.

Volcanoes—Openings in the surface of the Earth's crust through which lava, gases, and ashes are forced out.

Water vapor—Droplets of moisture floating in the air as fog, mist, or steam.

SUGGESTED FURTHER READING

Asimov, Issac. *Solar Power.* New York, NY: Walker and Company, 1981.

Baines, John. *Conserving the Atmosphere.* Austin, TX: Steck-Vaughn Library, 1989.

Becklake, John. *The Climate Crises.* New York, NY: Franklin Watts, 1989.

Bilger, Burkhard. *Global Warming.* New York and Philadelphia: Chelsea House Publishers, 1992.

Cross, Mike. *Wind Power.* New York, NY: Gloucester Press, 1985.

Cross, Wilbur. *Solar Energy.* Chicago, IL: Children's Press, 1984.

Dolan, Edward F. *Our Poisoned Sky.* New York, NY: Cobblehill Books, 1991.

Gay, Kathlyn. *Ozone.* New York, NY: Franklin Watts, 1989.

Greene, Carol. *Caring for Our Air.* Hillside, NJ: Enslow Publishers, Inc., 1991.

Hackwell, W. John. *Desert of Ice—Life and Work in Antarctica.* New York, NY: Charles Scribner's Sons, 1991.

SUGGESTED FURTHER READING

Johnson, Rebecca L. *The Greenhouse Effect: Life on a Warmer Planet*. Minneapolis, MN: Lerner Publications Company, 1990.

Koral, April. *Our Global Greenhouse*. New York, NY: Franklin Watts, 1989.

Miller, Christina G., and Louise A. Berry. *Acid Rain: A Sourcebook for Young People*. New York, NY: Julian Messner, 1986.

————. *Jungle Rescue: Saving the New World Tropical Rain Forests*. New York, NY: Atheneum, 1991.

Milne, Louis J., and Margery. *Nature's Great Carbon Cycle*. New York, NY: Atheneum, 1983.

Murphy, Bryan. *Experiment with Air*. Minneapolis, MN: Lerner Publications Company, 1991.

Peckham, Alexander. *Global Warming*. New York, NY: Gloucester Press, 1991.

Perrin, Noel. *Solo: Life with an Electric Car*. New York, NY: Norton, 1992.

Pringle, Lawrence. *Global Warming: Assessing the Greenhouse Threat*. New York, NY: Little, Brown and Company, 1990.

————. *Antarctica: The Last Unspoiled Continent*. New York, NY: Simon & Schuster Books for Young Readers, 1992.

Stille, Darlene R. *Air Pollution*. Chicago, IL: Children's Press, 1990.

————. *The Greenhouse Effect*. Chicago, IL: Children's Press, 1990.

————. *The Ozone Hole*. Chicago, IL: Children's Press, 1991.

AIR ALERT

Tesar, Jenny. *Global Warming.* New York, NY: Blacklunch Graphics, Inc. 1991.

Young, Louise B. *Sowing the Wind.* New York, NY: Prentice Hall Press, 1990.

SOURCES FOR MORE
INFORMATION

Acid Rain Foundation
1410 Varsity Drive
Raleigh, NC 27606

Argonne National Laboratory
Building 362-2B
9700 South Cass Avenue
Argonne, IL 60439
(For information on the Junior Solar Sprint)

CAREIRS (Conservation and Renewable Energy Inquiry and
Referral Service)
P.O. Box 3048
Merrifield, VA 22116

Center for Renewable Resources
Dept. REC
Suite 638
1001 Connecticut Avenue, N.W.
Washington, DC 20036

Environmental Data Service
National Climate Data Center
Ashville, NC 28801

General Motors Electric Vehicle Program
Government & Public Relations
P.O. Box 7083
1450 Stephenson Highway
Troy, MI 48007-7083

League of American Wheelmen
190 West Ostend Street #120
Baltimore, MD 21230

National Aeronautics and Space Administration
John F. Kennedy Space Center
Kennedy Space Center, FL 32899

National Arbor Day Foundation
100 Arbor Avenue
Nebraska City, NE 68410

National Center for Atmospheric Research
Information and Education Outreach Program
3450 Mitchell Lane, Building 4, 1st Floor
P.O. Box 3000
Boulder, CO 80307-3000

National Energy Information Center
U.S. Department of Energy
1000 Independence Avenue, S.W.
Washington, DC 20585

National Tree Program
America the Beautiful Program
USDA Forest Service
Urban and Community Forestry
201 14th Street, S.W.
Washington, DC 20250

SOURCES FOR MORE INFORMATION

Northeast Sustainable Energy Association
23 Ames Street
Greenfield, MA 01301
(For information on the American Tour De Sol)

Public Information Office
California Air Resources Board
P.O. Box 2815
Sacramento, CA 95812

Rainforest Action Network
450 Sansome, Suite 700
San Francisco, CA 94111

Solar Brigade
National Audubon Society
950 Third Avenue
New York, NY 10022

Sunrayce Headquarters
National Renewable Energy Laboratory
409 12th St., S.W., #710
Washington, DC 20024

U.S. Environmental Protection Agency
401 M Street, S.W.
Washington, DC 20460

U.S. Windpower, Inc.
6952 Preston Avenue
Livermore, CA 94550

INDEX

Note: Page numbers for illlustrations are in italics